D0961379

VIKING
Mystery
Suspense

# TOUGH Baby

# JESSE·SUBLETT

*Viking*

VIKING
Published by the Penguin Group
Viking Penguin, a division of Penguin Books USA Inc.,
375 Hudson Street, New York, New York 10014, U.S.A.
Penguin Books Ltd, 27 Wrights Lane, London W8 5TZ, England
Penguin Books Australia Ltd, Ringwood, Victoria, Australia
Penguin Books Canada Ltd, 2801 John Street,
Markham, Ontario, Canada L3R 1B4
Penguin Books (N.Z.) Ltd, 182–190 Wairau Road
Auckland 10, New Zealand

Penguin Books Ltd, Registered Offices:
Harmondsworth, Middlesex, England

First published in 1990 by Viking Penguin,
a division of Penguin Books USA Inc.

1 3 5 7 9 10 8 6 4 2

"Who Put the Sting on the Honey Bee," by Jesse Sublett.
© 1988 Big Striped Cat Music, BMI. By permission
of Big Striped Cat Music.

LIBRARY OF CONGRESS CATALOGING IN PUBLICATION DATA
Sublett, Jesse.
Tough baby / Jesse Sublett.
p.   cm.
ISBN 0-670-83325-8
I. Title.
PS3569.U218T68   1990
813'54—dc20       89-40690

Printed in the United States of America
Set in Times Roman

To Lois

## ACKNOWLEDGMENTS

For certain tips, riffs, and inspirations, I am obliged to Lois Richwine, John "Scooter" Schmidt, Rick Beatty, Jon Dee Graham, Johnny Reno, Jake Riviera, Teresa Garrett, and Richard Luckett. I'd also like to thank Lisa Kaufman at Viking Penguin, Abigail Thomas of the Liz Darhansoff Literary Agency, and Richard Green of the Lynn Pleshette Agency.

This book was written under the influence of Howlin' Wolf, Muddy Waters, Willie Dixon, Robert Johnson, Lou Ann Barton, Stevie Ray Vaughan and Double Trouble, the Fabulous Thunderbirds, and Bryan Ferry.

# TOUGH Baby

# Intro ...

There were four people in the room. One was a doctor, one was a comatose girl, one was a homicide detective, and one was a rhythm and blues bass player being held for suspicion of attempted murder. The room was cold. My knees shook. I was the bass player.

The girl's chocolate brown skin made the doctor's hand appear sickly white as he felt her cheek. Machines were hooked up to her, bandages were wrapped around her head. Her eyelids were as black and swollen as plums.

The doctor gave us a nod and Detective Sergeant Jim Lasko took me out into the hall. A nurse walked by, doing a double take when she saw the Austin police department badge clipped to the pocket of his Hawaiian shirt. The shirt accentuated rather than disguised his beer gut and just barely hid the leather holster on his hip. Lasko shook his head slowly as he tugged on the short hairs of his beard with the callused fingertips of his right hand. He played bass guitar, too; I'd even given him some lessons. "Well, Martin," he drawled, "you aren't the only one of your combo who got himself in trouble last night. One of the other dicks said your guitar player was almost cited for disturbing the peace early this morning."

I just shrugged.

"You don't seem surprised."

"Lasko, I just spent eighteen weeks on the road with Leo Daly, and no, I'm not surprised at anything he does anymore. He can play the hell out of a guitar, but he's definitely a couple of bricks' shy a load. I don't know what's gotten into him."

"Well, you know what they say about people who live in glass houses. We'd better talk some more about what happened last night."

We walked down the hall together, two men from very different lines of work with a couple of things in common: a love for rhythm and blues and an attempted-murder case. We found a place to drink coffee and sit down. What I really wanted was a dark, quiet corner to lie down in.

# 1

For the most part, it had been a good gig. It was nice to be back in our hometown again, and the Continental Club was packed, especially for a Sunday night. Maybe they'd missed us. I was wearing my black vintage suit, playing my candy-apple Fender Precision bass, as usual. The four of us played loud and tight, showing off our road muscles while keeping the arrangements lean and tough.

The first set went smoothly. We liked to warm up with a song list built mostly around Al Green and Wilson Pickett classics— ones that the saxophonist, Ray Whitfield, really shined on. Our second set was generally more hard-boiled and raunchy, consisting of some of our originals and whatever vintage material struck our fancy that particular night. Lately that meant a raft of rocked-up Howlin' Wolf and Muddy Waters. And that was Leo's chance to really cut loose on guitar and vocals.

During the last song before our break, I happened to glance back at the drum riser just a split second before a splintered missile flew past my right eye. Billy had broken a drumstick. He whipped a spare out of his quiver without missing a beat, not even losing the ash off the end of the Kool screwed into the corner of his scowl. I looked over at Leo, who was bent over his Stratocaster, coaxing a high wail out of his treble strings, lost in solo land. Ray hadn't noticed the near miss either. He was standing coolly on his corner of the stage, his black hair so severely slicked back that it looked painted on.

No need to get surly just because I nearly lost an eye and no one noticed. I thumped my bass a little harder, tilted my head back, and took a deep breath. My bags were still in the van, packed. My girlfriend and her eight-year-old boy were in the audience, and I hadn't had a chance to tell them hello. We'd rolled in from Baton Rouge at a quarter to ten, just enough time to wolf down some chips and salsa while the two roadies set up the gear. Then we took the stage for the first set and they stepped out. At first I assumed that they'd gone to the sandwich shop next door to get us something to eat during our break, but a dozen songs later, there was still no sign of them.

The crowd cheered Leo on as he executed a sizzling pick-slide down the fretboard and started chugging out the final refrain like a true R & B road warrior. The tempo picked up, Ray kicked in, and the crowd whooped and whistled louder. They didn't care that our nervous systems were jangled, that we were tired and hungry, or that our guitar player had set fire to a dressing room in Baltimore, trashed motel rooms in three states, and disappeared with the van for almost twenty-four hours in New Orleans and never told us where he went.

At the moment, I didn't much care, either. After the song ended, I put down my bass and stepped off the stage. Ladonna was making her way back.

I gave her a great big hug, drinking in the smell of her hair and the feel of her body pressed close to mine. She made a sound in my ear, and then we kissed.

"Hi, Martin," said a young boy's voice. Ladonna and I broke apart enough for Michael to give me five. I stood back and looked them up and down, up close for the first time in eighteen weeks. Ladonna DiMascio, a broad-shouldered platinum blonde Italian, stood a head shorter than my six feet. Her dark eyes locked onto mine, and she smiled a smile that tingled my road weary muscles. Michael stood with his hands stuffed deep in the pockets of his Levi's, the sleeves of his black T-shirt rolled up, the laces of his Converse All Stars undone, the way all the kids were wearing them.

"Sounds great, Martin," said Michael.

"Thanks," I said.

"It's good to see you," she said.

"It's good to see *you*," I said. The usual gold hoop earrings dangled from her earlobes, and her porcelain white face bore the usual knowing expression. She wore a short emerald green vintage jacket with padded shoulders, and a tight-fitting miniskirt. "You look great. In fact, you look extra great."

"You look like you lost some weight," she said, "but you look good." I could tell she was looking at the dark circles under my eyes. But she wouldn't say anything about that. Not right now.

"Look," I said, "I think we're playing till a little after two, then I have to get paid and we might have to load the van up ourselves because the roadies disappeared after sound check—"

"It's OK," she interrupted. "We have to go. Tomorrow is Monday, and I have to be at work early and Michael has school."

"I still have a key."

She shook her head and squeezed my hand. "Not tonight, Martin. I'll see you tomorrow, after work."

I was disappointed and I let it show.

"I'm sorry, Martin. I tried to take tomorrow off but there's a big deal going on at the office. They even tried to get me to work tonight."

"Well, I hope my cat is glad to see me."

She smirked and ran her fingers over the stubble on my chin. "Martin, you know you won't be out of here before three or four. People will want to buy you drinks, or somebody will try to sell you a guitar. Or something. I know how it is."

I reluctantly agreed that she was right and walked them back to her car, kissed her good night, and came back inside to check the tuning on my bass. Still no sign of Nick and Steve, our AWOL roadies. But Ray was in the dressing room with his girlfriend, Kate. In a Chanel-esque suit and leopard print pill-box hat, she was perched atop a road case giving Ray a list of phone calls that needed to be returned. When we were off the road Ray had paying gigs almost every night, sometimes with several different bands. I asked him if he knew where Leo was.

He ran a finger across his pencil-thin mustache and shook his head. "He and Nadine came back here a couple of minutes ago. He bit her on the neck and stuck his hand up her skirt and she slapped him. Leo went out to the bar. I think she left."

Leo had lived with Nadine ever since he'd sauntered into a diner at three in the morning with no shoes on and couldn't remember where he'd left them. Kate padded up to him in her cute little waitress uniform and greeted him with the "no shoes, no shirt, no service" line, and he answered with, "No shit, huh, how about a date, then?"

He was a lanky, tawny-haired guy who wore white T-shirts and jeans and tennis shoes. Religiously. Some people said he looked a lot like James Dean, and he had the kind of goofy charm that made you either forget or forgive most of his she-nanigans with a roll of his big blue eyes and shrug of his bony shoulders. And most of the time he *was* either charming or harmless.

I had worried about him and a couple of times had tried talking to him about his antics on the road. But the road is not a great place to put things in perspective. Living on a vampire's schedule, eating at truckstops, and making a living by making noise that made people move funny and ingest large amounts of alcohol, tobacco, and other things that weren't necessarily good for them, it was easy for him to shrug his shoulders and say, What do you mean, crazy?

Suddenly the dressing room door swung open and there he was. He slapped me on the back and spit a guitar pick out into his palm. "Hey, Martin," he drawled, "how 'bout a couple shots of Jack Daniel's before we fire up again?"

The last set had five Howlin' Wolf tunes in it that really smoked. Leo growled out the lyrics with edgy authenticity and Ray honked out the harmonica phrases on his saxophone. It was only May, but the air in the club was so hot and close that my suit had become a soggy mess pasted to my body. Nearly every face in the club was bleary-eyed and goofy. Neon glinted in their eyes like the last live coals in an old fire. An elderly black man jelly-walked his way up front, tipped his beret at me, and mouthed, "Not bad for a bunch a short-haired white boys." Some couples snuggled in the back, ready to go home. Other pairs looked surly with mischief, ready to get it on in a stall in the restroom, if they hadn't already. After-hours businessmen checked their pagers one last time before heading out the door or up to the bar for that last cocktail. Billy pounded out a drum roll to signal the end, and we blistered out the last twelve bars of the last song, a rumbling assault of sound that brought the house down and the lights up.

But the crowd on the dance floor wanted more. They stomped and clapped and whistled, even after we were back in the tiny dressing room, toweling off. Rings clanged against longnecks, boot heels clomped, glass broke. Texas crowds are the best. Leo abruptly slung his Gretsch semi-hollowbody guitar over his shoulder and headed back out. We followed him up on stage and watched as he rolled his volume knobs up to ten. Billy and Ray looked at me for a sign, and I looked at Leo for one. He rested one of his size twelve sneakers on a monitor and let the guitar squeal feedback for a painful fifteen seconds, then launched into a psychedelic blues version of "The Eyes of Texas." We couldn't play along with it, the crowd couldn't dance to it, and only the hardiest could stand it.

It emptied the club quicker than a DEA raid. I wished I'd tried a little harder to talk to him on the road.

---

After we loaded up the van, Wayne, the club manager, came backstage and handed me a stack of money. "One thousand nine hundred ninety-five dollars and seventeen cents," he said, grinning widely. "Broke your guarantee by almost a grand. Welcome back home."

"Thanks." I moved over to where the light was better and sorted out the cash into various denominations on top of a beer crate.

"Your bar tab was on the house. You guys were really hot tonight. Playing all those one-nighters sure punched up your sound."

"Thanks again."

"But that Leo, I don't think his parachute is packed right. You better keep an eye on him."

"I will. Leo's just been acting up. I don't know why."

He nodded and scratched his head, reaching around to check the short ponytail in back. I went back to counting.

"One more thing you might wanna know," he said. "The manager of Raven's down on Sixth Street? He said your roadies, Nick and Steve, come high-tailing it through his club behind two Mexican girls just before midnight. He said the girls were all decked out in biker gear, but your roadies were naked." He bellowed out a laugh and then shrugged. "Think it's true?"

I just gave him a blank look. It could be. From out in the club, someone was yelling, "Leo, get your ass down from there!"

"Made you lose count, didn't I?" said Wayne. "Count it tomorrow and let me know if I shorted you. You know I'm good for it. Come on out to the bar when you're ready. It's a friend of mine's birthday and I got the doors locked. Drinks are on me."

There were fifty-one twenties, three tens. That left a lot of fives and ones. I was looking for the calculator in my bass case when I felt a draft. Along with the draft came scents of perfume and leather. I looked up and saw a chocolate-skinned beauty with her hands on her hips, smiling a one-sided smile.

"Bitchen suit," she said. "Makes you look like a gangster."

The first thing you noticed was her hair. It swelled up into a bubble on top, not as extreme as a beehive, but retro chic. Five foot five in black leather jacket, black western shirt with pearl buttons and white piping, tight black jeans, conch belt, boots. The half smile seemed like a promise of something better, or maybe just mischief. I liked her.

"In fact," she went on, "your whole band looks like a gang of bank robbers from some black-and-white movie."

"Are you a reporter?" I asked.

Her laugh was a tinkling sound, like ice tumbling into a high-ball glass. "No, I'm not. I'm a detective, and I love the blues." She extended a hand. "My name's Retha Thomas."

"I'm Martin Fender," I said.

"I know. Can I buy you a drink?"

"Drinks are free."

"How about a cigarette, then?" she said, tapping on a pack of Camel nonfilters. My old brand. I took one and lit hers with the Zippo I still carried out of habit and respect for tradition.

"Aren't you going to light yours?" she asked.

"No," I said, sniffing it, rolling it around between my callused fingertips. "I quit."

She nodded knowingly. I stuffed the still-uncounted cash into my jacket and followed her into the bar.

It was already after three a.m. The band, the regulars, and a few characters I recognized as coke dealers, managers, and people with a nose for dropping in at the right place at the right time were singing happy birthday to someone I didn't know. Leo sang the worst.

I was glad to be back in Austin, but I still felt like I was in transit. I had a scattered feeling, like I was the victim of some sort of new age baggage foul-up, with my head still in New Orleans, my feet in Dallas, my fingers in Birmingham. Only my luggage had found its way to Austin, and it was still packed, sitting in the back of the van. I searched out the faces of the band members in the mirror behind the bar—Ray Whitfield, Leo Daly, Billy Ludwig, and myself. We all had that look, that thousand-yard stare. We'd get over it.

It's a long strange road out there—vans break down, club owners try to stiff you, and there aren't many good enchiladas. Up through the crawfish circuit and the swamps and the backwoods of the delta where the blues was born, through a hundred Denny's and over the interstates dodging methamphetamine-crazed truckers and sadistic highway patrolmen, up the East Coast through the gray slush of the last winter snow, playing the dives and college pubs and even a couple of hyper-trendy underground dance clubs in Manhattan, then trickling back through Ohio and Michigan and Illinois, Kansas, Nebraska, and Oklahoma, grinding down frets and popping strings, eating breakfast at four a.m. in truckstops and getting kicked out of motels—we had been on the road and it had been on us. It did something to you. It made your hometown look like a strange town, like something you remembered from a dream. It made every bar seem the same. Because over all the miles and through all the drinks and the thick smoke and local chatter, some things always *were* the same. The music was the same. You pulled into town and people got plugged into your music, then you packed up and either split or stuck around for a few drinks and—until I'd quit—cigarettes, finding out that the people who had danced to your music were pretty much the same, or you went back to the motel. And motels were pretty much the same. When you live on the road, life is a road, and the people you encounter are pit stops.

She looked good to me.

"I hope you don't think I'm trying to pick you up," she said. She had fake fingernails, as unrealistic as birds' beaks painted red and glued to her fingertips. But for some reason, they suited her.

I shrugged. "I've got a girlfriend."

"The girl with the kid who was here earlier?"

I nodded. "Ladonna. With Michael. Eight years old and he's my most brutal critic."

"Maybe you're just a wimp, or you haven't run into that many critics."

I laughed. "Oh, I've known a few. I think he prefers more modern stuff. And I'm not his father."

"She's really pretty."

"She is. She's got to work tomorrow."

"You probably sleep till noon."

"You're a good detective. What are you working on?"

She smiled that half smile. The way it bared her eyeteeth suggested a possible cruel streak. Or maybe she was just trying to keep from smearing her teeth with lipstick. "I heard there's a party. It looks like this one's winding down."

"I don't know." I looked over at the bartender. She was running a rag over the bar with a look of finality. The beer chests were padlocked.

Retha Thomas pointed at the cigarette I held close to my lips. "You gonna have a relapse? Light one up for old times' sake?"

"I don't know."

"There's a jam session going on at the party. I heard that the band down at Antone's was gonna head over there after their gig."

"Eddie Shaw and the Crows?"

She nodded. I hadn't jammed with the Crows in almost a year. Over in the corner, Leo had just told a bad joke. People were laughing anyway.

"Let's go," I said.

I put my bass in the trunk of her rented Ford and we went to the party. It was in a three-story house in Travis Heights, a rolling, shaded section of town just south of Town Lake. It was also no more than a fifteen-minute walk from my apartment on South 1st Street. Something to bear in mind, I thought, as we entered the raucous throng in the foyer. Disco music blared away at ear-splitting levels.

We wormed our way through the crowd, trying to sniff out the liquor supply as we were carried along by the noisy current of hot flesh, twanging voices, smoke, and sloshing drinks. Before long we were out on the patio in back. A band was playing. The next thing I knew I was yanked up onto a makeshift stage. A clunky Japanese bass guitar was thrust in my hands, and Eddie winked at me and played a riff in E and the rest of us kicked in. The night air was heavy, and with the crowd hemming us in on all sides I was soon blowing pearls of sweat off the end of my nose. I don't know how many songs we played. Some were Wilson Pickett songs, which I did not mind in the least. Some were mindless three-chord party jams, and those were OK too. After thirty minutes or so, a bass player I recognized got too close to the stage and I shoved the bass in his hands. I hopped off the platform, straight into the hot and sweaty embrace of Retha Thomas.

It was like an electric shock.

We clung. Two sweaty bodies colliding together will sometimes do that. She'd been dancing. I gave her a salty kiss. At first it was just a mindless thing, a reaction to our sudden collision, but then it took on a mind of its own, plunging deep and long as the humid mass of humanity pulsed around us. For a few seconds we were somewhere else, in a cheap motel room in a naked, sweaty knot—then a couple of drunks jostled us and we broke apart. I took her arm and we made our way through the dancing mob, back into the house, back into the disco music. I tried to avoid her gaze and brush off the sudden eruption of passion as just one of those things, but it was a halfhearted effort at best. My body throbbed for her.

"I could use a drink," she shouted in my ear.

"Wait here," I shouted back. She smelled like sweat and leather and perfume, and my face was wet where it had touched hers. She winked at me, and I think I winked back.

I threaded my way toward the kitchen. It seemed that a

couple of hundred Austinites weren't worried about getting up and going to work tomorrow morning. Surely one of them could tell me where they were hiding the liquor. After an expedition that took a good ten or fifteen minutes, I came back with a couple of Styrofoam cups of Jack Daniel's and ice. In the meantime, though, someone had given her a margarita.

I combined the two whiskeys and we toasted. "To the detective business," I said.

"To the blues," she said.

We stood in the shadow of a hulk of welded scrap metal. It looked like a dinosaur skeleton mating an oil derrick. She'd been in town a couple of weeks, she told me. "Working on what?" I asked. "You never said."

"And you never told me what kind of relationship you have with your girlfriend, or," she said, fingering my lapel, "where you buy sexy suits like this."

"We've gone out for a couple of years. I have trouble discussing our relationship on postcards and long-distance phone calls. It's no easier doing it now at a loud party with a stranger." As if to prove my point, the music got louder. It was some sort of decadent dance music, martial drums and synthesized kazoos. Nascent bubble gum vocals. At least they had liquor.

"It must be hard, being on the road, having a girlfriend."

"Hard? It's crazy. But I'm crazy about her."

"She'd be crazy if she didn't try hard to work things out. You're very handsome, Martin. The way you handle that bass, so tall and thin in that suit. It's really cool. Where'd you get it?"

"I got it at Vick's Vintage," I said. "There are a couple of other good vintage shops around, if you're interested."

I didn't think she was, actually. But her expression darkened, and she said, "I've heard about Vick. I get the impression he's quite a character. And every time I drive by his store, it looks like it's full of musicians."

"This *town* is full of musicians. And it's full of characters. Vick happens to keep a good stock of vintage guitars and amps as well as clothes. People go by there to check out the inventory, shoot the bull, be seen. The thing you have to bear in mind is that this is Austin. There are more than seventy-five live music clubs, but there's no big music business. It's all cottage industry, a big flea market. Lots of clubs and small record labels. Critics, promoters, singers, bass players, songwriters, guitar players. Lots of guitar players. Any night of the week there's bound to be a dozen clubs that have a guitar player on stage who could be the next Eric Clapton, but he couldn't tell you the area code of a major record label. In this town, a guy with an answering service and a Fax machine is a mogul. Vick Travis is a big fish in this little pond."

"That tells me something about Austin," she said. "But that's not really what I meant about Vick being a character."

I didn't answer her. Someone had just collapsed next to me and knocked my drink into the sculpture, smashing the Styrofoam cup, drenching my suit. The culprit had friends. They helped him get vertical as I gave him my smashed cup. A guy with a Neanderthal face, short black hair, and an oversized head on a small but raw-boned body in a vintage black tuxedo came over and asked them if they needed any help taking him out. They took one look at his leering face and said no. He gave us a backward glance as he disappeared into the crowd.

"Speak of the devil," I said, "that was Vick Travis's right-hand man, Ed the Head."

"I know. He gives me the creeps." She shivered. It made her breasts jiggle.

I looked her up and down and bit my lower lip. My body was full of road aches and unsatisfied needs. The music didn't help. The volume and beat combined with the lights demanded that you give in. Nobody just stood and listened to that stuff. It was dance or fuck off.

"Damn," she said. "I think I lost an earring."

"Probably happened when that moron fell on you," I said. "I'll look for it." I got down on one knee and scanned the floor.

"Oh, just forget it," she said. "It's just a Melrose Avenue trinket."

Something sparkled down there. I scooped it up just before a heavy-soled boot would have come down on it. As I raised back up, my head hit something.

"Ow!" she exclaimed, cupping her face with her hand. Blood seeped out between her fingers. A giant knot twisted hard in my stomach.

"I'm sorry. Do you have something?"

"Here," she said, handing me her drink. She dug in her purse and got out a wad of travel-size Kleenex. I put the drink down and helped her as much as I could.

"I'm really sorry," I said. But in a loud, hot room full of fumes of drugs, smoke, and alcohol, *sorry* was a very small word. She didn't try to make me feel any worse, though.

"It's all right. My nose bleeds at the drop of a hat." She daubed it with the Kleenex and looked up at me. That half smile again. Blood glistened on her jacket and dotted my white shirtfront. The strobe lights made the dots dance and change colors.

"I'm jumpy," I said. "I need a cigarette. And I still haven't had a drink."

"You can have mine," she said.

I took it and had a gulp. "Would you like to leave?"

She nodded. We started threading our way through the sea of hairdos and elbows and uncertain feet. I didn't think the tequila and the whiskey would go together on my suit, so I gulped it down before I got slammed again. It was like swallowing a sledgehammer.

I never liked margaritas.

The ceiling looked familiar.

The view through the sliding glass door out onto the parking lot and the creek that was below it looked familiar too, even though I was seeing it sideways. Sideways and blurry. An ugly haze seemed to cling to the couch I'd slept on, the sideways fat striped snoring tabby, TV, stereo, thrift shop dinette, and refrigerator. This last sideways item was buzzing quite loudly.

Down a short hall and to the left was a small room where I had a desk and guitars and amps, to the right was the bathroom, straight back was the bedroom, which was too hot to sleep in during the hot months. The cat was in the middle of the living room floor, lying on his back, which was how he slept during the hot months.

I was home, and I was a bundle of pain. From my throbbing head and burning eyes and ringing ears to the elephant's foot on my chest and the bucket of molten lead in my stomach. From the hot steel pincers on the back of my neck to the dull rawness of my gums. I tried to get up but the molten lead sloshed in my stomach and the steel pincers pinched harder and deeper. The phone had been ringing.

Now someone was knocking at the door.

---

The next thing I knew Lasko was standing over me, shaking his head, rubbing his beard.

"Looks like you all but burned up on reentry," he said. I was in no condition to look at the large Hawaiian shirt he was wearing. There seemed to be palm trees swaying and waves cresting on it, and that did my nausea no good.

"Go 'way," I said. "I don't feel good."

"You don't look too hot either, Martin. Where's your bass?"

"It's too early for a bass lesson, Lasko. Come back tonight. I know I owe you a couple of sessions, but it's too damn early."

"It's three in the afternoon. And I didn't come over here as one of your students. Not even as your friend. I came over here as a cop."

I managed to get one elbow under me and tried to focus on his face. He wore a gimme cap with a beer company insignia on the crown. His curly reddish hair was a little long for a cop but not for a plainclothes homicide detective sergeant. He was frowning.

"I was hoping at least that your bass would be here," he said.

The nausea was taking on a life of its own. It moved in a wavelike motion, churning, trying to tell me something. I swung my legs off the couch and managed to get up, shakily. Where *was* my bass? "Hang on a minute," I said.

I stumbled down the hall and leaned inside the office. My spare was in there, but not the Fender. It wasn't in the bedroom, either. I had a hazy recollection of jamming at a party. But I'd played someone else's bass. Some Japanese model with computer age electronics and a neck like a two by four. Ugh. Where was my bass? I wouldn't have left it at the club . . .

Back in the living room, Lasko hadn't gotten any cheerier.

"Know a girl name of Retha Ann Thomas?" he said.

"Yeah," I said. Things were starting to move around in the fog. At first they were just shapes, then they became people, events, places. "I met her last night. I guess I left it in the trunk of her car."

Lasko was shaking his head. He used the toe of one of his cowboy boots to pry one of my shoes out from under the couch, then jerked his head at me. "She's in a coma with a caved-in head down at Brackenridge ICU. Somebody bashed her up good with a P-bass. Looks an awful lot like yours."

"No." Now I was going to be sick. The carpet seemed to turn to quicksand under my feet. I might never drink again.

"Goddamn, there's blood on your shirt."

"I can explain that."

"Get your shoes on," he said.

"We've got statements, Mr. Fender," said the Lieutenant. He looked at me with his bulldog face, twiddling his thumbs over his abdomen. He was flabby and jowl-ridden, old at fifty-five, without an ounce of humor. He was smart as a whip but would act dumb as a rock if that worked better. "Statements that say you really tied one on last night, though I can guess that for myself. Statements that you were with the girl at the bar, that you went with her to the party in Travis Heights. But you can't say where you went after that party."

"I wish I could," I said. "I just can't remember."

It was a small room and the blinds were drawn. The Lieutenant manned a desk. Lasko sat in a chair to the side of it. I sat in a hard wooden chair, gulping hot bitter coffee, wishing it were all a dream.

"All right, let's back up," said the Lieutenant, looking up from a folder. "It doesn't say here where you work."

"I'm a musician."

"We *know* that." There was cruel sarcasm in his voice. The bass had turned out to be mine.

Lasko cleared his throat. "Uh, Lieutenant, Fender here is pretty much a professional musician. Though he does work part-time for a collection agency as a skip tracer."

"Hmm. That right?"

I nodded.

"Not all that professional, then. What's the name of the agency?"

"Lone Star Detectives," I said.

*"Detectives?"* He thought it was grimly humorous.

"Yeah. They have a private investigations part, and then there's the collection agency, which I work for. When I need the extra money."

He nodded at Lasko. "That why you've been in trouble with the law before? I see we have some notes on you. One of your roadie friends and you were running around town with a guitar full of cocaine, and people seem to have followed you around falling down dead. You have some kind of fascination with crime, Mr. Fender?"

"I'm just a musician, sir. I almost make a living at it. The skip tracing covers the 'almost' part. I've been in trouble before, but I don't generally go around looking for it."

"This guy actually helped bring the guys in that did it, sir," said Lasko. "A guitarist friend of his had been apparently killed over the coke. It was back—"

"I don't give a damn about all that, Sergeant," said the Lieutenant. "A couple of Fender's roadies cut a swath of terror through the Sixth Street area last night, and his guitar player was up on top of the American Bank building just before dawn howling like a gut-shot dog, so I don't care to hear any glowing character profiles just now. Let's concentrate on the business at hand." He decreed that there would be a few seconds of silence by slowly turning his head to one side until the bones in his neck popped, then slowly turning the other way, apparently gazing at something somewhere above my head as he pushed a stack of Polaroids across the desk to me and nonchalantly said, "Sure you don't remember?"

I looked down as the pictures fanned out, at first not realizing what they were. Glazed garish splashes of color in the intervening darkness gradually came into focus as objects my brain could catalog. A black girl on a stretcher, bloodied and swollen.

A motel room, with patches of dark discoloration and huge swashes of blackish red on the sheets. Blood. Wreckage. A candy-apple red Fender Precision bass guitar, the metallic finish smudged and dark, on the bed where her unconscious body had been found.

"Robbery was not a motive, and it appears she was raped," said the Lieutenant. "We're not certain if it was before, after, or during the beating. We'll know more later on this evening."

He looked up as the door behind me opened. He nodded, then motioned to Lasko. The two of them got up to leave. The Lieutenant paused in the doorway and said, "Be back shortly. Try to jog your memory a bit, maybe we can clear this up. Make yourself at home."

I didn't like the way he said it.

When Lasko came back he sat in the same chair and gave the Lieutenant's desk the same kind of deference as when his superior had been sitting there. Maybe even more so. His face was lined with tension. He said, "Christ, Martin, you really fucked up this time."

"I just had a couple of drinks to unwind after a gig, like I've done a million times. I didn't do anything wrong. I just can't remember what I need to remember to get me the hell out of here."

"Know anybody who can verify that you accidentally bloodied her nose at the party?"

"I'll try to remember."

"Well you do that, then." He sighed hard. "Hell, I know you weren't trying to pick this girl up. Not consciously, anyhow. I know you and Ladonna got a good thing going. But maybe Retha Thomas didn't know that."

"Meaning?"

"I don't know, man. Girls just seem to bend over backward for musicians, that's all. And you getting so whacked out of your mind isn't helping matters any. You start doing dope on the road or something?"

"Hell no. I never touch the stuff. You *know* that."

"Well, maybe I do. You do like your Scotch, though."

"Scotch never did this to me. Give me a urinalysis."

"What for?"

"I think I was drugged."

"Oh, come on, Martin."

"You want to solve this, or not?"

He just scowled and looked away.

"Lasko, look. I told you that I drank her drink. That's one of the last things I remember. She said she was a detective. Maybe she found out something she wasn't supposed to find out. Maybe I ended up with the Mickey Finn that someone intended for her—"

"Or maybe you were s'pose to get it and this is all a big frame-up. Aw, come on. They already tried doing a remake of *D.O.A.* Filmed it here in town. Even with Dennis Quaid, it was a bomb. It ain't gonna go over any better now."

"You can't rule it out. She said she was—"

"She was unemployed. Hadn't had a job in three months. Before that she worked for a record store in LA, Tower Records. We checked with the people at La Quinta Motor Inn where she was staying and it doesn't appear she even knew anybody in town. Just here for a vacation, apparently."

"If she dies and the autopsy turns up a drug and you keep me down here much longer your chance of finding out if it's in my system goes down the drain. As a matter of fact—"

"All right, all right. Might as well let you piss in a bottle. Least that way we get *something* out of you."

And that was how we ended up over at Brackenridge Hospital, looking at Retha Thomas in a coma. Lasko had hoped that she would have regained consciousness and would be able to vouch for me. No such luck. Also, after my urine sample was sent down to the lab, Lasko wanted to personally talk to the lab people at Brackenridge to make sure everything was coordinated properly. Retha had had at least a sip of that margarita.

It was a waiting game. Her parents were flying in from LA. The doctors were waiting for a change. They said she could go either way. The DA was waiting, too. If Retha came to, they could ask her if I was the one who beat her up and ripped her clothes off. If she died, I was a murder suspect. The stakes would be higher. They could hold me for several days without bail while they gathered evidence and decided what degree of murder charge to file.

I wanted to get out of there before her parents arrived. I wanted her to live, I wanted to know what happened after I drank that margarita, and I wanted someone to pay for what they did to her.

I was almost as annoyed with Martin Fender as Lasko and the Lieutenant were. I felt dumb, numb, and guilty. Maybe it was the hangover talking, but whatever it was, it nipped and nagged at me until it became a nagging chorus with another thing that had been bugging me for eighteen weeks, something I hadn't done anything about.

# 3

It was almost eight o'clock when Ladonna's black Ford Escort pulled up in front of the hospital. As I walked down the steps, I couldn't see her face, only one porcelain white arm and shoulder, a charm bracelet on a slim wrist, and long red nails tapping the steering wheel. I could still hear Lasko's words.

"Aside from your bass being the weapon and her blood being on your shirt, it's circumstantial evidence. But pretty heavy circumstantial evidence that might get a helluva lot heavier between now and tomorrow. Thing is, you're a well-known character about town. That gets you in free to all the clubs. It gets you a bit of recognition on the street, gets you strange women wanting to give you a ride to parties. For chrissakes, you been around the music scene forever, you oughta get something out of it. But the Lieutenant doesn't give a rat's ass about any of that, it's less than circumstantial. You can't put it in the bank, you can't take it to court. Might be the only thing it gets you is one last free night . . ."

They said her skull was cracked up like an egg, and there were internal injuries, too. Things didn't look good. Ladonna knew it. I could see that. Feel it too.

She wore a Day-Glo green tank top and white Capri pants

with a wide black patent leather belt and sling-back shoes. With her hair combed off to one side, you could see that she had better bone structure than Madonna. But that face bore a stern look now, modulated by a slightly quivering chin.

"Welcome home," she said as she whipped the car out into traffic, cutting across a couple of lanes of 7th Street to get on the interstate. She hadn't kissed me, hadn't even touched me. And I didn't press the matter. "Billy dropped off your bags. I'm taking you to your place. I can't leave Michael alone for very long."

"He doesn't know."

"Of *course* he doesn't know," she snapped. "By the way, he said to tell you again that you were really good last night. I had a hard time getting him out of the club. It *was* good. But he can't be out all night, and even though things are usually pretty slow at the real estate office with the economy the way it is around here, I have to work, you know. If only I would have stayed, and . . . oh, *Christ* . . ."

She jerked the steering wheel, lurching the car onto the off ramp. She took the serpentine curves of Riverside Drive even faster than usual, sailing through the amber light on South 1st, going left, up the hill and into my driveway. She parked under a big oak tree, set the brake, cut the ignition, and hunched over the wheel, crying.

To my surprise, she didn't push me away when I tried to do something about it. She still sobbed, chewing on the knuckles of a slim hand knotted into a fist. Without looking up she said, "I guess I'm just feeling sorry for myself. All I know is I'm trying to decide whether I should paint the bathroom in the condo pink and I get a call from Lasko making you sound like a dangerous criminal and he's making me promise that I won't let you do anything else stupid and all I can think is I'm almost thirty and I don't need this shit."

"Nobody does," I said. "Paint the bathroom pink and you can hang that velvet Elvis Presley in there. I'll do it for you. Let's go talk."

It was awkward. Even making drinks was awkward when it should have been a normal thing. A couple of Scotches on the rocks can be the most normal thing in the world, but the world had changed an awful lot between now and that last margarita.

And the drinks helped only in the telling of the tale, not in accepting it. When I was done, she leaned back and looked stunned. "I can't believe it, but I'm taking this personally," she said. "You've been in trouble before, but so many times it was because you were trying to help someone out, or you were hanging around with some of your weird friends and some of their troubles became your troubles. But this time, Martin, this time it really seems like you did it to yourself."

"Why? How? All I did was go to a party with a semistranger. Maybe my troubles are connected with that decision, but I can't imagine how my decision is connected with what happened to her. And why is it that Lasko thinks he can trust me, but you want to blame me?"

"She was beat up with your bass, Martin. Maybe Lasko thinks he knows you, but I know you well enough to know that you don't leave your instrument in strange places. You're very careful with that thing. But I suppose if you were messed up enough to be careless with that thing, then maybe . . . Oh, God, I hate this."

"Ladonna . . ."

"I mean, hell, you took a ride with her. If your bass was in her room, then *you* must have been, and . . ."

"I'm not sure if you're more worried that I might have almost killed her or that I might have had sex with her."

Her face went red. Every muscle in her body seemed rigid. I moved a little closer to her on the couch, and when I reached out to touch her, she shot straight up. *"Don't touch me,"* she hissed.

"They're doing tests—"

"Oh, shut up," she said. Her voice was icy, hard.

The building shook when she slammed the door.

---

I knew I hadn't done anything wrong. I just wanted witnesses. Almost as bad as I wanted a cigarette. I mean, I wanted one *bad*.

It was stupid. Suddenly my decades-long addiction to smoking was foremost on my mind. It seemed to symbolize the whole situation. Everything seemed cloaked in a blue smoke haze. The road trip. Being back in town. Being a musician.

Three weeks into the road trip I got a scratchy throat that turned into a stubborn throat infection. I thought about cancer, I thought about mortality, I thought about getting older. I thought about the possibility that I might not get much older if I didn't give up cigarettes. And my singing voice, never much to begin with, was getting hoarser. Giving up cigarettes seemed like the right thing to do. So I did.

Right away I became less tolerant. Sound checks that dragged on longer than they should became a supreme irritation, rather than just one of those things. Brain dead promoters struck me as candidates for flogging. Critics, whom I'd never had much patience for, got less and less of my time. And Leo. I had to wonder if his antics had gotten worse, or I'd just gotten less tolerant of them.

Maybe it was my age. I didn't worry about smoking six years ago, when I was almost that many years away from being past thirty. Maybe I was just older, and less tolerant, period.

Cigarettes still seemed like a good idea. The situation I was in would be so much easier to sort out with an ashtray, a lighter, and a cloud of smoke in the room. Cigarettes give you attitude, atmosphere. And cancer.

My throat felt fine again. But I was losing my mind.

I was just headed out the door to buy a pack when I saw Nick walking down the hall. He was shaking his head, roadie's flashlight stuck in the pocket of his motorcycle jacket, a cigarette dangling from his lower lip.

Nick had blond hair down to his shoulders and the heavyset,

blockish build common to a lot of roadies. When he was bent over, hooking things up, the back of his jeans usually drooped low enough to show the elastic band on his underwear. "You wanna know what the hell happened?" he said gruffly. "I'll tell you what happened. We got fucking held up by a couple of Latina biker chicks is what happened."

"I don't think I've heard this one before," I said.

"Go ahead, laugh if you want. They said they'd give us a ride down to the club if we'd get them in free. Said their bikes were parked back in the alley behind one of the new discos off Red River and Sixth. I swear there's a dozen new ones opened since we left town.

"So we follow them back to the alley and that's when one of them pulls a .357 Magnum and says free up your cash. We did, then they made us strip so we wouldn't chase 'em."

"But you did anyway."

"Damn right. They were a couple of tough babies. But we chased after them when they headed back for Sixth Street. Hell, we didn't think they'd shoot us in front of all those people cruising the strip. We would've caught those bitches, too, but a couple of beat cops nabbed us right outside of Raven's. We had to spend the night in jail. I called you, man. How come you didn't come down and bail us out? Haven't you checked your answering machine?"

"I've had problems of my own." I told him about them. The knockout cocktail, the girl in a coma, the circumstantial evidence . . .

"Damn," he sighed. "I'm sorry. Anything I can do?"

"I'll let you know."

"Sure thing," he said, stubbing out his cigarette. "Say, I was wondering if me and Steve could get an advance on the next gig. I know we missed last night but it wasn't our fault . . ."

I gave him a couple of twenties out of the Continental Club pay. "Try to stay out of trouble, OK?"

He started out the door and gave me a funny look. "You'd better talk to Leo, Martin. I really think he's losing it."

After Nick left, I sat down with my thoughts for a while. Leo had always been a little zany. Up until this last road trip he'd seemed, if anything, slightly manic depressive. Sometimes he'd brood for days inside his house, not venturing outdoors unless it was for a gig. Then he'd play guitar like a house on fire. I didn't worry about him then.

Politicians have to be a little crazy, comedians have to be a little crazy. So do musicians. Leo and I had discussed this at length late one night as we drove from Columbus, Ohio, to New York City. Driving such a long distance between one-nighters makes irony a constant companion. Philosophy comes easy. Because what were rock and blues and jazz after all? What was music to us was always noise to someone else. You dedicate your life to something that is basically noise. Is that crazy or what?

The people I played with were fanatics for the blues. The blues had evolved more or less directly from traditional African music, the call-and-response chants of slaves in the fields, and the gospel singing of the poorest of the poor black cornfield workers in the Mississippi Delta. It was the legacy of black Americans, but we were hooked on it, too. The guys in this particular band may have been white, but we didn't identify with whitebread America either. Being born white and middle class didn't mean we had the keys to the castle, and although we stood more chance of ending up with jobs on Wall Street than a kid from the ghetto, it was just as unlikely.

So there we were, making a living making noise, arranging that noise in patterns that were the heritage of another race. Thus were our obsessions and our occupations intertwined. We knew we were a little crazy, and we knew we weren't getting rich, not any time soon. But we liked our work, and there was nothing else we'd rather do. It was, as the song goes, nice work if you can get it.

So we arrived in New York City after that long drive, and spent the whole cold February in a Winnebago parked on the edge of Manhattan, playing Max's Kansas City, CBGB, and a slew of other clubs in Manhattan and other places within a half day's drive. The Winnebago was much cheaper than a hotel, but it was cold and cramped. We spent a lot of time huddled on the top of the Winnebago sharing a cheap local brand of whiskey. I forgot the name, but not the motto: "Only the finest, since 1974."

One night the stars managed to peek out through the murky sky as Leo and I polished off another bottle.

"You know, when I was a kid," he said, "I used to shoot at the moon and stars with this little .22 rifle. Take real careful aim, you know, and fire away. I thought I was bound to hit one of them. The moon was a lot easier target, but there were so many more stars, I figured I had a better chance hitting one of them. I knew they were a long ways off, but I had no earthly idea how far, and I didn't know how far the gun would shoot."

He shook his head, grinned, and took another slug of whiskey.

"Don't you feel a whole lot older and wiser now?" I said.

He tilted his head back and took in the view. "Not as many to shoot at here. Think kids who grow up here know what they been missing?"

"I doubt it."

"Thing is, Martin, sometimes I'd have a sort of a pang. I'd think, shit, what if I hit one, and the thing goes down? What if I did get a bull's eye on the moon, and the damn thing comes falling out of the sky? You know what I thought?"

"Thought you'd get in trouble, I bet."

"Well, the only thing I could think, that the damn thing would come crashing down right on top of my parents' house."

"Then you'd be in trouble for sure."

He laughed. "Yeah." He sniffled, bunching up inside his parka. "Ain't that something? Now why would I think it would land on top of my parents' house, instead of somebody else's?"

"You were a kid, Leo. Young and dumb."

"Yeah. Never dreamed I'd be up here in West New York in a trailer park, freezing my ass off, playing for a bunch of goddamn yanks whose idea of showing their appreciation for a band is to put their drinks down once in a while so they can clap once or twice. Audiences suck here, man."

"I definitely prefer the whooping and hollering back home. I don't think I've heard more than one or two people whistle after one of your lead breaks the whole time we've been here. But it's good exposure. Who knows, maybe they'll run our picture in *Interview* again."

"Yeah, whatever. I guess we're lucky to be gigging. A lot of bands can't even get a weekend gig in their hometown. Here we are, in a situation a million kids would give their right arm to be in, and we're complaining about the audiences, the weather . . ."

"Their lousy excuse for Mexican food . . ."

"No ice tea refills . . ."

"MTV brats who never heard of Howlin' Wolf . . ."

"But the bars stay open later, and the pizza's a hell of a lot better."

"They've got the Chrysler Building, and we'll be home in a few weeks."

"Yeah," he said, cracking a smile. "I'm starting to like that Caribbean food they got here, too. It ain't Seis Salsas, but it kinda tickles my spice gland. Might as well bone up, keep on doing what we do. We do do what we do, do we not?"

"That's right. If you're a musician, you gotta make music. And we're a long way from your parents' garage."

"That's right," he said. "And the moon never fell on it, so I guess I'll just keep on shooting."

I took Nick's dirty ashtray out on the balcony. Even though I'd been dying for a cigarette just minutes before, the urge was gone and the sight and smell of used ones was annoying. I'd deal with cigarettes and crazy guitar players later. Right now I needed to get back to trying to piece together what had happened in my blackout period.

I caught my next-door neighbor just before he went to bed. He'd fed the cat and kept an eye on the apartment while I was on the road. But he hadn't heard me come in last night and couldn't say if I came home alone, unattended, or if I just beamed down from the Starship *Enterprise*.

I called the guys in the band. Leo was out. I called Nadine at the diner, and she said she hadn't seen him. He hadn't come home last night and when she went out to the store and came back he'd dropped off his stuff and left again. She said it looked like he'd bought a new guitar. That would make thirteen.

Kate said that Ray had a gig, which was no surprise.

Billy's answering machine didn't say where he was, but I figured he was down at the studio, and it turned out the answering machine was on there, too.

I tallied up the rest of the Continental Club money and looked over the road ledger and tally of charge slips. It looked like Sunday night's pay would just barely cover the bills that would be coming in.

I made myself another drink. It didn't taste right. Even the cat was avoiding me. I went into the bathroom and looked at myself in the mirror. I drank the drink and still I didn't look any better. I realized I hadn't showered since I'd gotten to town. I showered, shaved, and put on a clean white shirt and some trousers that still had creases in them. Thin white socks, black faux alligator shoes. A skinny black belt with a deco buckle.

Ten o'clock at night, no cigarettes, what does a potential rapist-murderer do next? Sitting around, watching TV, waiting for the phone to ring with reports from the police lab would only ruin the creases in his trousers. Damn, I thought, I've got to do something.

Time to prowl.

I pulled the rain cover off the Karmann Ghia, folded it up, and stuffed it in the boot. Low slung, sleek, retro, it was a 1970 convertible with a fresh coat of what the paint shops call Texas yellow. All the dings had been taken out, including the small dent in the nose, which was now perfectly rounded again. I gave it a little pat, admiring its streamlined face. The vents in the nose were its slanted nostrils, the headlights staring out from the sweeping front fenders were its eyes. It had upwards of 150,000 miles on it and it fired up right away.

I rolled out the drive onto South 1st and headed south toward La Quinta Motor Inn. There was just enough cool and damp to the air that the neighborhood fragrances carried in the breeze, and it seemed that my head was finally clearing as I made the uncomplicated cruise of the near South Austin neighborhood around Bouldin Creek, a cozy old shoe of narrow streets and sprawling oaks, tire swings in yards and a high density of Mexican food restaurants. The average resident was either a blue-collar worker or a musician, or both. I swung east on Oltorf across the interstate feeling no nostalgia, only an overwhelming need to pick up no clues that belonged to me at the motel.

It didn't feel familiar. The desk clerk barely looked up as I crossed the lobby. I went out through the glass doors into the swimming pool area. I walked around until I saw the room on the second floor roped off with yellow crime scene tape. The lights were on.

I took the stairs up to the second floor, walked down toward the room like I was a guest, and peeked in through the window. Two cops in almost identical brown suits were wrapping things up. The walls were still splattered with blood, not the bright red stuff you see on television and the movies but the ugly dark-hued stuff that really is blood, flung into cross-hatched patterns and dribbling smudges that left a horrifying dropcloth blueprint of violent frenzy.

I thought about how I'd accidentally bloodied her nose and my stomach immediately knotted up. I recalled that the incident had had a sobering effect. Standing there in a house full of people, hot and sweaty with a strange girl who was not my girlfriend, I had asked her if she was ready to go, then downed that margarita in one gulp. So where did I think we were going when we left?

The walls, door frames, double bed, TV, recessed vanity, table and chairs were all smudged with fingerprinting powder. The radio was on, playing "Stairway to Heaven." Her bags were parked by the door. One of the brown suits held open a large shopping bag while the other dropped a string of costume jewelry beads into it like a dead snake. I caught the name of the store on the shopping bag: The Discount Aristocrat.

I checked my watch. There was a good chance that Carolyn, the proprietor of the shop named on the bag, was still at work. She usually closed at ten and liked to have a couple of dry martinis while she waited for her husband to pick her up. It was no accident that I knew this information. I was a regular customer, and I'd found that this was the time to get a real bargain.

"Stairway to Heaven" was just climaxing on the car radio as I fired up the Ghia, and neither Led Zeppelin nor bargain hunting was foremost on my mind. I sailed over Oltorf, then wound up on Lamar Boulevard and turned left toward Clarksville. I killed the radio, preferring the screeching wails of my tires to those of Robert Plant.

"I agree with you, Martin, she didn't seem the type," Carolyn said, her voice a pleasant West Texas twang as she set her martini glass down on an end table that was a thick tinted glass top mounted atop the head and hands of a scantily clad ceramic Egyptian dancer. One copper-colored breast had popped out of the dancer's bustier and she didn't have a free hand to put it back in. "But I take whatever customers I get. All kinds of people come in here and buy stuff to wear to a costume party, or a gift for one of their token weird friends. My regular clientele, people like your saxophonist, they come in and spend a couple of hundred every other month on Bakelite or doggie bone sofas. Ladonna gets a lot of stuff here, too. You know that. If not for them, I wouldn't be in business. But that walk-in trade, the people who do ninety-five percent of their shopping at the malls, their money is green, too. So I don't care if they're the type or not. But there *was* something strange about her."

We were sitting behind the counter of her little storefront on West Lynn. Shafts of moonlight shot past the racks heavy with old suits and cocktail dresses, shelves packed with big chrome toasters and espresso makers and martini shakers, glass cases with Bakelite kitchenware, and rotating racks of wide silk ties, hand-painted.

Carolyn was in her late thirties. She used to breast-feed her son Ransom, now twelve, at concerts at the Armadillo World Headquarters, the old National Guard Armory that had been a sort of counterculture chamber of commerce back in the '60s and '70s. She'd seen a lot and forgotten little.

"I thought maybe she was picking up some souvenirs to take back to LA," she said, taking another sip of the martini, smacking her lips, "since she seemed like she was strictly Melrose Avenue—off the rack and a little dated. The thing I've noticed about LA fashion, Martin, is that they get a hold of a style and they don't let go of it for two or three years. That death-rock look, and the biker-cowboy thing. And boots. They really like their boots. But she's cute, and I kinda liked her. I tried to get her interested in a mink wrap, or one of those Joan Crawford padded shoulder jackets, but she didn't go for them. She kept coming back, though. She'd hang out, ask about things and about people around here. She'd usually buy a little something, but I never figured her out."

"She said she was a detective," I said.

"Well"—she laughed—"maybe so. Maybe she was investigating the thrift shop business."

"She ask about your business, or about any of the other stores in town?"

"Well, mostly about old Vick. She seemed pretty curious about him. I'd tell her what I know about Electric Ladyland, St. Vincent de Paul, Room Service, and Flashback, but she'd always come back to asking about Vick. I guess he does have the most interesting place in town." She finished her drink and stood, smoothing out the folds of her hand-painted muslin *china poblana* skirt as headlights swooped over us through the front window. "Ransom's here, and it looks like my husband's letting him drive, too. Can you believe it? Nice talking to you, Martin. Buy something next time."

I was starting to feel better and worse at the same time. Better, because my head was clearing and so was the situation. Worse, because it didn't make me like the situation any better. Retha Thomas had asked me about Vick Travis and how he was supposed to be some kind of character. She also told me she was a detective. At the time, it all seemed like after-hours chatter, the kind of thing that someone says and you play along with it. If you had more important things to talk about, you'd probably do it somewhere else, during a different time of day.

Lasko didn't seem very interested in the detective angle. He had plenty of other angles to keep him busy. However, it was one of the few things I had to go on, and, besides, Vick's muscle man, Ed the Head, had been at the party. Maybe he knew something.

I sped down 12th Street east toward the Capitol building, admiring its hard pink granite double dome bathed in respectful lights on a lap of cool green grass and surrounded by pecan trees, memorial statues, and silent cannons. I swung right on Congress Avenue, a corridor of brassy postmodern pyramids that elbowed out the older nineteenth-century structures, hogged the sidewalks, mostly stood there vacant—Johnny-come-latelies in the '80s boom that had gone bust. Downtown was quiet.

As I waited at the light at East 1st Street, the green mossy smells of Town Lake drifted over, cool and clinging. From where I sat, you couldn't see the litter and scum floating on the surface or hear the wicked undertow swirling below, and you might mistake the bats fluttering around the streetlights for sparrows. When the light changed I took the left and pulled over just past the Sheraton Crest. Vick's Vintage sat in the shadow of the hotel parking garage, a two-story flat-roofed yellow brick shoe box on the rise off the north shore of the lake, with no other concession to style than a curved wall of glass brick on either side of the front door now gray with street grime. I parked behind an olive green late '70s Plymouth with a blistered, peeling vinyl top and bondo spots on the trunk. There was a vaguely human shape in the doorway of the store, apparently locking up. I bounded out of the car and trotted up the sidewalk.

It wasn't Vick Travis, it was Ed. He always seemed to be at a doorway—working as a bouncer in a bar or working security at a concert. He worked cheap and was good at bouncing troublemakers, but he was scary looking and occasionally he bounced people too hard. Consequently, it was the sleazier bars and the more shakily financed concerts that employed him. He was shaking his head, using a mop handle to point to the "Closed" sign. I was tapping the glass with my keys, trying to shout through the glass that it was important, when a car engine suddenly roared to life and tires screeched. I looked back toward the street. Nothing remained of the Plymouth but a cloud of blue smoke. Someone had been in a hurry, someone who'd had his head down when I pulled up behind.

If Ed the Head cared about the quick departure of the customer in the Plymouth it didn't show on his face. Abruptly a dark bulky shape blotted out the light in the entranceway behind him. The dark shape loomed about a foot taller and a hundred and fifty pounds bigger than Ed. Inky shadows dripped down from the stone ledge of brow on Ed's face and danced from side to side as the shape I recognized as Vick Travis reached around and turned the key in the door. They made a scary-looking couple, the three-hundred-pound man with his arm around the hundred-and-fifty-pound thug.

I came inside and Vick looked me up and down as if I were the weird-looking one. He creaked as he moved in the extra-

extra-large black motorcycle jacket, mopping his forehead with a red bandana, coaxing back a corkscrew of dark hair. "Well, what is it, Martin? Break a shoelace before a big gig? Your bass amp blow up on you? What the hell is the emergency?"

"Retha Thomas is the emergency," I said.

"Never heard of her," he said. As he stepped back to give me a few inches' breathing room, he hit me with a suspicious look. But there was something vaguely conspiratorial about it, like a cigar store owner with some Havanas in the back that he's dying for you to ask for.

"Well, she heard of you," I said. Ed was uncomfortably close, fingering the mop and glowering as if I were standing on the last spot of floor that needed to be mopped. I gave him a look and said, "Do you know where I went after the party last night?"

He shook his head. "I left before you. Came straight over here."

"That's right, Martin," said Vick. "We had a little party of our own."

"Then neither of you know what happened to the black girl I was with?"

"Only the gossip we heard tonight from a couple of customers," said Vick. "You're the first one mentioned a name. What's it got to do with me?"

"That's what I'd like to know," I said. I scowled at Ed. He scowled back.

"Hey, Eddie, you get the bathroom done yet?" said Vick.

"Sure," he said in a dull baritone.

"You mop it good, Eddie?"

"I swabbed it, yeah."

"Well, check it again, OK?"

"Whatsa matter, Vick, 'fraid you left something in there?" When Vick didn't answer, he shrugged and ambled off, saying, "I'll check it and then I'm outta here." When he was gone, Vick motioned for me to follow.

The store was a terrific cluttered hell of overflowing bins of used clothes, racks of leather jackets, rows of tweed, polyester, herringbone, and houndstooth, shelves stacked with appliances, dishes, records, books, and junk with vague or unknown purposes and origins. I followed him into the back room, where dozens of old guitars hung from hooks like the carcasses of slaughtered animals. Moonlight poured in off the tinfoil lake through barred windows, enhancing the effect.

Vick sat down on a carpeted ledge below the guitars, wheezing from the effort of walking from the front of the place to the back. He propped one boot on the edge of an old Gibson guitar amplifier and mopped his forehead again. "Tell me about it, Martin."

"This girl you say you never heard of came to town, asked a lot of questions about you, then got beaten to a pulp and left for dead. Whoever did it used my bass. They didn't rob her. But someone slipped a dose of elephant tranquilizer in a drink I ended up drinking and I think it was intended for her, so that makes it look like it wasn't just a random assault, either. You see what I'm getting at?"

"Let's pretend I'm stupid, OK. Might save time. Why don't you tell me where this truckload of bullshit is headed."

"Like I said, she asked a lot of questions about you. Ed was at the party. Let's pretend *I'm* stupid. Why don't you tell me how these things might fit together."

"Man, I'm just a junk salesman. Why you trying to dump all this in my lap? Some Jane blows into town and takes the wrong guy home with her—what does that have to do with me?"

"She was raped too, more than likely, Vick. My blood type is B positive. I wonder what yours is."

"I'll be glad to tell you, you buy something."

"Like what?"

"Oh, say a pack of strings. You use those Rotosound roundwounds, don't you? Gimme twenty-five bucks, I tell you my blood type."

"I'll give you something else, you fat son of a bitch."

"You feel froggy, Martin, go ahead. Jump." He folded his

hands over his belly, closing his eyes and tilting his head back so that the fold of his extra chin disappeared. The old notion of fat people being jolly came to mind. Vick was too strange for the word *jolly* to fit. But there was something unformed and boyish about his big round face. The fat seemed to inflate all the details out of his expressions, making them seem like child-like curves drawn on a ball of dough. He was smiling now.

I wanted to slug him but I didn't. He leaned forward and backhanded me playfully on the stomach. I didn't like it.

"Martin, do I look like a rapist?" he said, holding his hands out to his sides, emphasizing his bulk. "She wasn't squashed flat like a tostada, was she?"

"This is not a joke, Vick. And you haven't answered any of my questions."

"Go to hell or Hollywood, man. You ain't the police. I told you I was here. I don't hardly go out anymore anyway."

"And Ed was here with you. After the party."

"That's right."

"That's very convenient. Especially since we both know Ed has a temper."

"Fuck you, man. I'll talk to the police, straighten this shit out. While I'm down there, I'll ask 'em if they checked you out properly. They'll tell me, too. Vick Travis been an institution in this town a long time. I'm big, man. Ha ha ha."

I could hear him still laughing as I went back through the store.

"I'm *big,* man," he bellowed. "I'm big as shit."

I went home and moped. The cat crawled up in my lap and rubbed against me, breathing asthmatically, his eyes big and round as marbles. I wasn't sure if he was trying to give or receive sympathy. It didn't much matter. I called the police station a couple of times, but Lasko never came to the phone. I called his trailer, but there was no answer. I called his beeper, but no one called me back. There was one message on my machine, from Billy, returning my call. Call me tomorrow, he said, he was going to bed. He felt like the road was catching up to him.

I got back inside my jacket and walked down to the Continental Club to catch last call. Other than the bartender, who gave me a couple of drinks on the house, there was no one there who could help me. I thought about Ladonna and wondered if she was awake, and, if so, if she was thinking about me. Those thoughts got me nowhere. I bought a pack of cigarettes and lit one for Retha Thomas. It wasn't a candle, but I wasn't Catholic. I set the cigarette in an ashtray and watched the smoke curl up from it, hoping that she'd be OK. When there was nothing left but a slim finger of ash, I put the pack in my pocket and walked home.

"Hello?"

"Martin?"

"Lasko? What is it? What's the word?"

"I'm sorry to wake you, Martin. It's Jeff LeRoy. I've got a gig for you."

"Uh . . . I'm sorry. I just dropped the phone. I was expecting another call. What's the deal?"

I supposed I'd gotten two or three hours of deep sleep and a couple of hours of unpleasant horizontal time, eyes peeled back, cold sweat, shaking hands, ice cube toes. I accepted the gig and digested the details pretty professionally, considering the fact that my frayed nerves were taking to raw wakefulness like a naked person diving into a snowdrift.

The gig was a part of the local chamber of commerce's efforts to help out the music scene. They felt a bit guilty after relentlessly promoting the type of economic development that reaped a bumper crop of skyscrapers and microchip consortiums at the expense of skyrocketing downtown rents that forced a lot of clubs to shut down. The guilt came after the real estate boom went bust and the new buildings stayed empty and the industries they wooed with tax concessions and university endowments skipped out of town. Then someone did a survey and found out that most of the town's residents felt that—surprise—the Fabulous Thunderbirds, Antone's, and the Cannibal Club were just as important (if not *more* important) to Austin as IBM and Motorola. And a majority also felt that Austin had suffered a decline in the quality of life, one of the elements that had been loudly trumpeted in the brochures and portfolios used to lure industry and investment to Austin in the first place. Someone sensed a vicious cycle at work.

So the chamber of commerce was picking up the tab for air time on the local stations. Joe Ely had been scheduled to do a ninety-second spot—eighty seconds of music and ten seconds saying, "Get off the couch tonight. Turn off the TV and go see a band." But something had come up for Joe and we were going to do it instead.

I felt lucky that I was able to locate all three of my bandmates plus one of the roadies—Nick—and get them to agree to show up at the Channel 36 studio at one o'clock. Then I checked my watch: eight o'clock. It hadn't been luck; they'd all been in bed, like me. I'd have to call them later and remind them that it wasn't all a dream.

I had less luck getting in touch with Lasko. I called back and asked for the lab, but no one there would talk to me. I called Brackenridge Hospital. There had been no change in Retha's condition.

Ray and Leo were late as usual. Ray was consistently twenty minutes late. Leo could run from an hour to an hour and a half late, showing up only five or ten minutes late once in a blue moon just to throw off the average and to make you think that the rest of the time he just couldn't help it. The technicians were getting nervous, so they helped Nick unload and set up the gear. It wasn't like setting up a heavy metal band with walls of megawatt amps and double-bass drum kits or racks of synthesizers, tape machines, and flash pots. We were stripped down retro and proud of it. I used a customized Fender Bassman tube head and a cabinet loaded with two heavy-duty fifteen-inch speakers. Billy kept the beat with a kick, floor tom, two racks, hi hat, ride, splash, and, occasionally, a cowbell. To go with his thirteen electric guitars, Leo had about half that many amplifiers, though he never packed along more than two of them. Lately he'd been using a Pro Reverb. Nick had everything plugged in and tested inside of thirty minutes.

Leo straggled in at a quarter of two hauling a triangular guitar case with a pink tag attached to the handle. A new guitar. He set the case down, opened it, and slung a vintage red Gibson Flying V over his shoulder. He grabbed the guitar cord Nick handed him, plugged in, and said, "Hello, Martin. How you like it?"

With its flawless fire engine red finish on the V-shaped body, rosewood neck, and original square headstock, it was a beauty—the prototypical Albert King model. But what got my attention was the white plaster cast on Leo's right hand.

"Don't worry, man," he said, acknowledging my stare, "I can still play." He held up the cast. His index finger and thumb were still free, and there was a pick between them. "See?" he said, and slashed out the loud three-chord riff to "Mannish Boy."

BUH *BAAH* BAH DUM

In the key of E, it was the rudest, machoest musical figure that had ever been born. Leo slashed it out again.

BUH *BAAH* BAH DUM

You could almost hear Muddy Waters growl his fearsome testimony of elemental manhood, you could almost feel the sawdust on the floor. Leo Daly's mojo seemed to be working.

BUH *BAAH* BAH DUM

The cast was disturbing, but the guitar tone said it was all right. Leo's face said something in-between. The chords shook the room, causing toes to tap, heads to nod. That riff had been used in everything from real folk blues to burger commercials. It was a deeply rutted thing, second nature to rock and rollers and blues players alike, as basic as the missionary position, but like that tradition also, oh so serviceable.

Leo stood with his legs apart and slung his head back in a grimace, deviating from the riff by ripping into the strings with a series of quick runs up and down the frets. It wasn't flawless, and it wasn't the best he could do, but it would work. He let out a big sigh and wiped his hair out of his eyes with the cast-encased hand.

"What happened?"

"I fought the wall and the wall won."

"Was that after you were up on top of the American Bank building howling like a gut-shot dog?" I asked.

His grin died an ugly death. He unscrewed the top off a quart of Jack Daniel's, took a big slug, and set it on top of his amp. "Nope," he said. "It was before."

A couple of the techs had gathered around and they nodded and elbowed each other, impressed. They looked fresh out of college and, having been weaned on the excesses of the Stones and Led Zeppelin, they thought they were witnessing rock and roll attitude incarnate. But they were nervous, looking up at the studio clock every couple of seconds, then looking back at me and the empty spot on stage right where Ray's saxophone stand waited like a bride at the altar.

And then Ray sauntered in, cocky and sharp as Dick Tracy's jaw—straw racetrack hat, houndstooth suit, wing tips, black-and-white thick and thin socks. Every hair in place, his mustache actually looking as if it were drawn with a fine tip felt pen. His saxophone case was at his side and Kate was behind him, on high heels in a Chanel-esque suit and pillbox hat and tortoiseshell Ray-Bans, cigarette smoldering at a right angle between two black-gloved fingers, around her neck a round patent leather purse on a chain big enough to hold one large pill or maybe a silver dollar, but not both.

He put the case down, pointed to a chair out of camera range for Kate, and wrinkled his nose as if it had just detected a trace of drugstore cologne. He looked at the cameras and techs, then me. "Are you off the hook yet, Martin?"

"Any minute now," I said. "Once they get the lab results . . ." I let it trail off. Ray was smirking with amusement at Billy's casual green rayon shirt, the usual pack of Kools showing through the translucent material. As Billy rapped his snare like a judge banging a gavel, Ray gave him a wink, then glanced toward Leo, who was turning around from his amp, tuning up. When he saw the cast on Leo's hand, the perpetual sneer seemed to freeze in place, his lip quivering slightly, as if he were having a stroke.

"Leo—" I began.

"Let's just get on with it," snapped Ray, obviously irritated beyond any reason that I could see.

"We waited for you, Ray," I said. "You think we could wait for Leo to tune up?"

He regarded me coldly. "What you do with your time is your business. Right now it's my time, and no one's going to waste it, especially . . ." He paused and gave me a strange look. "Where's your bass, Martin?"

We finally got started. Stupid, stressed-out me: My P-bass was at police headquarters, a realization that was awful in both its timing and implications. The band members groaned a bit, but they were pretty understanding. Lasko had questioned each of them since yesterday. I had a spare, a Danelectro, but it was at home and we were already late. It turned out that one of the studio interns had a Gibson EBO-1 in the trunk of his car and he loaned it to me. Whereas a Fender Precision represents perfection in style and function, an EBO does not. Either burpy and muddy at best or muted and untrue at worst, it would have to do.

We decided on a song and proceeded to come up with an eighty-second segment that would work. We were a blues band and not a radio jingle band, so it took some doing. We never knew the length of any of our songs until they appeared on the local records we put out and we saw the times on the labels, but we never played them the same way again anyway. The song we picked for this spot, "Who Put the Sting on the Honey

Bee," was a hard-charging song with enigmatic lyrics that Leo drawled out of the side of his mouth, letting the inflections he used on the words reveal their true meaning. Like when he sang, "When I'm out of *luck,* late at night, the way you *touch,* treats me right . . ." the word *touch* sounded nastier than a word that rhymed exactly with *luck*. Not that he was above singing lyrics that left little to the imagination.

The song was in F# minor arranged around a slight deviation of the usual 1-4-5 twelve-bar pattern, and the crew was grooving to it, laughing, tapping their toes, miming applause when we wound it up. But when I botched the announcement at the end by saying, "Get off your *band* tonight, go see a *couch,*" no one laughed or clapped. They laughed the first couple of times, but not the fourth.

"We could do a voice-over," suggested the producer. "You're playing at Antone's Saturday night, right? We'll just tag that on the end. You guys just smile at the camera, or look tough, or whatever, after you hit the last chord. How about that?"

"That might do," said Ray. "Or Leo can do it. We don't want Martin telling people to come see us at Antone's, *blome* of the *hues.*"

A voice-over would be fine, we decided. Just before we did another take, Billy summoned me over to his kit. "Martin . . ." he said, and counted off the song, then played the beat, emphasizing the feel by elongating the spaces before the snare beat. He played a couple of bars, staring at me, bobbing his head along with it. "You see?" he said. "Like that. I know you've got something else on your mind. Just try, man, and we'll get out of here."

Leo came over and slapped me on the back. Ray was busy adjusting his reed. We tried it again.

Billy was right about other things being on my mind. I couldn't help it. It wasn't the bass. It sure wasn't the music. I'd played the song hundreds of times and played songs just like it thousands of times. The riffs were a part of me, the different modes and nuances being no different than words in a conversation. But when I glanced down at my hand around the neck, it looked like a fist holding a club. Someone had held my bass like a club and clubbed Retha Thomas almost to death with it. And that wasn't all they did. She was a girl I'd just met. A girl who, well, I'd thought was pretty good-looking at the time, hadn't I? Maybe I hadn't planned on going back to the motel with her, but I was just off the road and half crazy from it, maybe subconsciously I'd been thinking I'd just play it by ear, see what happened . . . That's not a crime. After all, Ladonna and I weren't married. But if I was just going to see what happened, then I got a hold of a drink that had been spiked, then what? Casual sex being OK, what about casual murder?

"Martin . . ." It was Billy.

Everyone else had stopped playing.

"You missed the change," said Leo.

My face burned red. "Sorry. One more time."

I put the thoughts out of my mind. Only the song, only the song would be on my mind this time. Billy gave a four-count and off we went. A crunching, sleazy beat. Greasy. Smell of barbecue, sounds of horns honking on South Congress on a hot afternoon. Guitar clank, saxophone growl. Billy kept it on that East Side cruise mode, and rumbles came from the bass in my hands, hands that I would not look down at. Leo sang, snarling . . .

> It's Saturday night and I got a right
> to a cocktail and a smoke
> the way she did that walk on me
> got to be a running joke
> money talks but love can sing
> every ache and every sting
> there's a lump in my throat
> and it's got a name
> I'd call her up but I'm ashamed
> guess you know that girl put my heart in a sling

Who put the *i* in satisfy
Who put the oooh in the *foo-ooo-ool*
Who put the flame in the three-alarm fire
Who put the boo in the boo hoo hoo
Who'd put a hex on a guy like me
Who put the sting on the honey bee . . .

And just beyond the too bright lights, Lasko walked in. I recognized his dark silhouette—the gimme cap, curly hair, beard, beer gut. Gun sticking out under a Hawaiian shirt, rocking back and forth on his cowboy boots. Then his hand came up, giving the OK sign. The rocking back on his boots, I knew, was for the music. The OK sign was from the lab.

I nearly blew the tempo as I sighed with relief, but jumped back on track before it was noticeable, and we climbed up to the high note, chugged it, then clanged the last chord, letting it die out until all you could hear was the buzzing of the tube amplifiers under the lights.

"All right, all right, all right," said the producer. "That's it. That's a wrap."

Given all the questions in the world that begged for answers now, even after getting a few of the most pertinent ones answered, why did I have to decide how I really felt about Michael Jackson?

Michael DiMascio wanted to know. And he didn't know about any of the other questions, only his own.

We sat together on Ladonna's soft sofa. She relaxed in the recliner. She'd had a hard day at work, and her time with me this evening had been no picnic. Michael had his mother's dark eyes and fair skin but his late father's dark hair, cut in a Beatle cut. On an inquisitive eight-year-old, it looked just right.

"Ronnie Gilroy says Michael Jackson is a fag," said Michael.

That was a tough one, too. I looked at Ladonna. She nodded at me, meaning that she wasn't going to offer any help. "Well, Michael, I doubt that Ronnie Gilroy knows that. Is Ronnie one of your school chums?" Michael nodded. "Well, like I said, I doubt if Ronnie would know that. Michael Jackson is very secretive about his private life."

He just sat there for a bit, knocking his Converse All Stars together. He looked from one side of the room to the other without moving his head. Then he said, "What's a fag?"

I looked at Ladonna. She thought I was doing fine. I said, "It's a guy who likes other guys. You know, instead of girls. They, uh, like to sleep together, but . . ."

"You mean they have sex together? They do it? Guys and guys? I thought only guys and girls could."

This was tough. "You already know about this stuff?" Ladonna was nodding.

So was Michael. "Ronnie Gilroy told me at school last year. He wrote 'Fuck' on the bathroom wall and I asked him what it meant. Then I came home and told Mom because I didn't know if she knew about it or not, because I never heard her talk about it. But she already knew."

Ladonna was stifling a laugh, in spite of herself. Too bad. It would have been the first time in at least a day.

Michael went on. "At first Mom was mad. Then she went and bought some books about it and told me all about that stuff. But I never heard about fags before today."

"Well," I said, "you probably shouldn't use that word, anyway, Michael."

"Why not?"

"Because, because it's a word that gets misused. You know how they say 'Sticks and stones can break my bones, but words can never hurt me'?" He nodded. "Well, that's only partially true, because sometimes people use words to hurt people. And a rock doesn't hurt anything, if it's just lying there, and a word doesn't hurt anybody if it doesn't get used in a bad way. But when people are, you know, sensitive, and they yell things at each other . . ."

"OK, I get it." He was nodding, leaning back on the couch with his hands locked behind his head. "You mean like how you and Mom were yelling at each other when you first got here tonight?"

Ladonna stood up. It was time for Michael to go to bed. He got the message and slid off the couch. "I'll come tell you good night in a minute," said Ladonna.

"Michael," I said, "I like Michael Jackson. But I think his last album was better than this one."

"Me too," he said, hands in his pockets, walking to his bedroom, a small man. Before he shut his door we heard him say, "Roland Gift is a better singer." Then the door shut, and we were alone. Sort of.

Her body was perfect.

She sat on the bed, arms locked around her knees, bathed in dim light from a lamp with a perforated black shade that cast protozoan designs on everything in the room, including us. She'd taken off her clothes and was going to take a shower before going to bed, but when she saw how I was looking at her she was faced with a decision: should he stay or should he go?

So I sat on the other side of the bed, and the satiny topography of the dimly lit sheets might as well have represented the Sahara Desert. Or the Antarctic. I felt that far from her. And it wasn't fair that she had to sit there so quietly with her feelings, so naked and beautiful and perfect.

And by perfect I don't mean to imply that she was some sort of human mannequin, either. Aerobics and an almost bottomless well of energy kept her firm and trim, but there were small traces of stretch marks on her breasts from having Michael, there was a vaccination mark on her arm, there was a little brown mole somewhere. But they just made her more appealing. Like tiny flaws in Michelangelo's marble. And knowing that I knew where they were and that I might not ever caress them with my callused bass player's fingers again, was causing me pain.

"So there was no semen in her," she said abruptly. "But there was a trace of someone's blood under her fingernails. What type was that?"

"O positive."

"And yours is B positive."

"Right. And it had a cocktail of Librium, Dalmane, Percodan, Demerol, Seconal, and PCP swimming around in it. Just like hers did, although I got most of the dose."

"And she gave it to you."

"Well, I don't think . . ."

"How long did you know her? An hour? An hour and a half?"

"Yeah. About an hour and a half." I didn't add that that didn't include whatever time elapsed after I drank the drink and before the time that she was attacked.

"So how could you know if she gave you the drink on purpose or not? Or did you know her before? Did you maybe go out in the parking lot for a blow job, a musician's handshake?"

"What do you mean by that?"

"You know damn well what I mean. I've heard your pals say it millions of times." Acidly sarcastic, she said, " 'To some girls sex is like a handshake.' " And pointing to her crotch, " 'Put her there, pal.' "

"I can't believe you'd even ask."

"I can't believe you'd answer with a bullshit response like that. Indignation is the first defense of a liar."

"Maybe so. But the answer is still no, and it happens to be the truth."

"But you'd lie to keep from hurting me. Wouldn't you?"

"Yes."

"And maybe you think you'd spare us both a lot of hurt if you were able to just gloss over the whole thing and pretend that whatever happened didn't have anything to do with you. But you can't remember, so you can't say for sure. Even though they didn't find your semen inside her and someone else's blood was under her fingernails, you were with her. What about fingerprints? They didn't find your fingerprints in her room?"

"They haven't been able to do anything with the smudges and partial prints they have, except to determine that none of them belong to me. I don't think I went to her room."

"You went to a party with her."

"I'm not denying that."

"Good." She folded her arms and looked at the wall. "Bastard. I trusted you. What about all those other nights?"

"I was faithful. For eighteen weeks I was faithful. I called you every few days, I sent you flowers. Last night I was tired and frustrated and a little drunk. You didn't have time for me so I went to a party with a girl. Something happened to her. I'm trying to find out what."

She didn't say anything.

"I won't give you up without a fight. If you don't want to try to work this out, if you don't think it's worth it . . ."

A big tear rolled down her cheek. Her eyes were all squinched shut, crow's feet forming in her smooth skin. She shook, all of her. I wouldn't have been human if I hadn't taken her then and put my arms around her and not let go. If I wouldn't have squeezed her tight, nestling her cheek next to mine, letting her bury her protests in the collar of my shirt. And I'm human.

We stayed together until my clothes were damp with sweat, her body warm and tender and still trembling just a bit, but yielding. She sighed.

"I'm sorry, Martin. I know I've been beating you up with this, holding it over your head, treating you like a suspect just because you were hanging around with her. I'm not worried that you would have hurt her. But I am jealous and angry and generally sickened that you're in this situation, and I just can't forgive you for it yet."

"I kind of figured that."

"It's been a long hot day, Martin," she said finally. "I'm going to take a shower. You'd better hang those clothes up or you'll never get the wrinkles out of them. I think you picked up all the clothes you had over here before you went on the road. Let me get you a couple of coat hangers."

"But that means I'll have to take them off."

"Uh-huh," she said.

She got in the shower and I undressed. I toyed with my cigarette pack for a while, thinking. Then the phone rang. I answered it.

"Martin?" said a tentatively aggressive voice. "This is Vick. Vick Travis."

"What do you want? Who gave you this number?"

"Your pal the cop."

"Even pals make mistakes. Good-bye."

"Now hold on. Hear me out. I figured he owed me since you tried to sick him on me this afternoon. Yeah, you hear right. I know you told him that gal was asking around about me. But I'm innocent as the goddamn pope. My blood type is A negative."

"OK. So maybe you didn't do it. Is that why you called?"

"Nope. I wanna hire you. Your boss at the collection agency tells me you got a nose for trouble."

"It usually seems to find me. I've had mixed results when I go looking for it."

"Come on, man, I'm serious. Dead serious. I got trouble and I can't afford a detective. Blackmail. Interested?"

"I'll call you back. I'm busy."

"Well . . ."

I hung up on him.

And then Ladonna came in the room and turned off the lamp. Her body was coolly damp. But warm. She trembled under my touch. We kissed. It was nice, but it didn't last long enough.

"Who called?" she asked softly.

"Vick Travis."

She pulled away. I kept our legs locked together.

"What did he want?"

"He wants me to do some work for him. He's being black-mailed."

"Blackmail?" She shivered. I could feel the bed shake. "He's gross, Martin. He's weird. Why doesn't he go to the police?"

"Why don't most people who get blackmailed go to the police? I don't know what it's about. I hung up on him."

"Sounds like you talked for a bit, though."

"Long enough," I said. I got on top of her. We kissed some more. She was quiet again, making soft low sounds, trembling a bit more under my touch, especially when I touched her breasts or her flat belly, and then she stiffened again.

"What are you going to do, Martin?" she said.

"What do you mean? Am I going to meet him, see what's up? I don't know."

"Martin. He's weird."

"I know. Can we forget about him?"

"No. And still, I keep thinking about the other thing."

"The girl."

"Yes."

"Try not to."

"I can't help it. Your touch, Martin, your body. It's so nice. It's so nice to feel it again, wanting it. But I can't help thinking, she probably wanted it too. And she might die thinking about it. It's not fair, Martin. It's a nightmare and I don't know if it's a real nightmare or just a thing, a thing that didn't happen. It's not fair."

"I know." I fell back on the bed, and she didn't cling. She laid there. I laid there. Vick Travis just loomed, a bloated presence there in the darkness, above the bed, above Ladonna's fragrance, above my guilt. Like the Goodyear blimp hovering over a game that the home team is losing.

"Did you kiss her?"

"What do you mean?"

"You know what I mean, you asshole."

I felt my face flush as I remembered that kiss. It was the kind of kiss that makes promises. It was even possible that part of me regretted not following through. If I would have, maybe she wouldn't be in a coma now. Possibilities came at me from left and right, none that would do us any good.

"Maybe I should just go. Get it over with."

She didn't answer right away. But then she said, "Yeah. Maybe you should."

"Goddammit. I told you I wasn't going to give up easy."

"You've fought pretty hard tonight. You're pretty hard to resist, actually. But the other thing . . . It's big. It's really big. But I'm trying, I really am. The thing is, I have to work tomorrow. I know that sounds trivial, especially to a musician, but I don't see this getting any more resolved tonight. I'm tired and it's *hard* to think. Maybe you should go. Especially if you think it could help."

We kissed good-bye.

We sat on folding chairs on either side of a card table in a dusty little cubicle that was heavy with cigarette smoke. A single bright bulb hung from a greasy cord. Bugs fluttered around it. There was a small wooden desk shoved in the corner with invoices, notes, and returned checks pinned to the wall. Keith Richard was nodding out in a poster tacked up by the door leading out to the guitar room. Vick Travis belched, then squelched it with another swig of Carta Blanca beer. He almost looked like he was going to say excuse me but didn't. It would have seemed too trivial.

I drank my beer and watched him smoke his fat, aromatic French cigarettes. It was time to get to the point.

"Maybe the girl was part of it, I don't know," he said. "But these guys, there seems to be two of them, they want twenty grand, and they want it damn quick."

"They going to burn your store down if you don't pay up, or what?" I said.

"Well, it's simple. It's kinda funny, the way it worked out. First of all, you know about these records?" He pulled a half dozen albums and EPs off the desk and plopped them down on the table.

I fanned them out. *Big Bad Wolf and the Blues Gig, Live.*

*Tammy Lynn Johnson. The Backstabbers. Cloud 19.* A couple of others. All either Austin groups or from the general area. All of them were on the R & R Addiction label, released locally in the late '70s or early '80s.

"R & R Addiction is my private label, Martin. You know that."

"Sure. Tammy Lynn's getting some action on the college charts now, isn't she?"

He nodded. "So are the Backstabbers, and they played Cloud 19's 'Solo Bolo' on 'David Letterman' the other night."

"Congratulations."

"The big congratulations are coming from IMF Records in LA. A hundred grand worth of congratulations. They're buying the label, and they wanna put out the catalog on CD."

"They're buying you out?"

"Yep. The copyrights, the masters, everything, lock, stock, and barrel. Besides the CD deal, they figure to recut some of the songs, repackage and do a rerelease, nationally. Whatever. I don't give a damn. They can do whatever they damn well please for a hundred grand. They can melt down all the stock and stick it up their butt, all I care."

"So how does that get you blackmailed?"

"Well, that's one side of the record—I've tried to keep the deal a secret, but this is a small town when you're dealing with the music scene, so evidently these boys, whoever they are, know I'm getting the money. The flip side of the record is this . . ." He flipped over the Backstabbers record and pointed to some fine white print.

"Danny Cortez, Executive Producer," I read aloud. "That's what you wanted me to see?" He nodded. "The title 'executive producer' means he put up the cash for making the record, right?" He nodded again. "And that name sounds familiar. Would that be Bingo Torres's old stage name, back when he was playing the teen canteens?"

"Yep," said Vick. "Bingo Torres, South Texas Payola King. Currently about a cunt hair away from federal indictment on the payola statute. He'll do time, too. Couldn't happen to a nicer guy."

"What's your connection?"

He shrugged, then spread his hands out expansively. "I've known him a long time, man. Like I know everybody, except this New Wave crowd. Back in the '60s he used to come in the Jade Room over on the East Side, peddling thirteen-year-old girls so he could afford to keep that band of his going. Wanted to be the brown James Brown. Ran peyote out of Matamoros for a while in hollowed-out Bibles. Then his uncle died and left him a radio station. You know how they got records played back in the '60s, man. It was the good old boy network, and we had a lot of Texas hits. Remember Mouse and The Traps, the Zachary Thaks? Thirteenth Floor Elevators, the Chains, Freddy Fender, Sam the Sham and the Pharaohs, Playboys of Edinburg, Sir Douglas Quintet? Tons of 'em. Hell yes. Well, Bingo got to know one of the indie record promoters, checked out his territory, how he did his job. What Bingo did, he found out what all these deejays liked, you know, as tokens of appreciation. It wasn't always nose candy or cash. One it would be a certain brand of whiskey, a single malt Scotch, real expensive, especially by the case. One liked black girls with real small tits. Another one had to have a new car every year. Bingo tallied up exactly how much money he'd need for six months' worth of juice, got a loan for that amount, and then went to the record labels and said, Hey, I can do this cheaper and better than you been paying these other guys to do it. They gave him a chance, and within a couple of years he'd built himself a regular empire. Not off those groups I just mentioned. They really were popular; they didn't need juice to get their records played. It was acts from the coasts, one-hit wonders looking for a comeback and lame, mob-backed artists that really needed him.

"You know, after Alan Freed got busted they passed some laws and everybody acted real shocked that stuff like that was going on in the music business, you know, like they thought that the reason something got played on the radio was because everybody *liked* it. Yeah, real funny. These things go in cycles. So Bingo saw the cycle coming and got out of the promo biz and went into real estate for a few years, made a pile of money, then got out before the oil glut knocked the bottom out of the real estate boom. He jumped *back* into record promotion, and he also paid for the pressing of a couple of my records here, using his old stage name. But those records flopped, and Bingo 'Danny Cortez' Torres don't gimme the time of day anymore. Let's talk modern history. You familiar with a record promoter named Mike Sigor?"

I nodded. "I think I met him once."

"Well, the feds probably got a picture of you shaking his hand in their files. They been dogging him for three years and they haven't been able to make a case, but last October they got lots closer than they been. What they did, they nailed a couple of smaller fry, a couple of indie promoters—Ray Ash out of New York and Craig Wilson out of Nashville. Both pleaded guilty to payola and criminal tax charges, but they're not gonna have to serve any time. Both used to work with Mikey Sigor, you see, and you can bet your ass that they ratted him out."

"You think they ratted on Bingo, too?"

He shrugged carelessly. "Who knows? It doesn't matter. Payola is the system, man. It's the only promotional system the record companies know. Once in a while somebody is gonna get thrown to the lions. But here's the feds, with the first two convictions on the payola statute in thirty years, and another one on the way. They've hit the East Coast and Nashville, and they're about to score on the West Coast with Mikey Sigor. I guess they figured they might as well get one in the Southwest market. Their blood is up, they come here, and they find Bingo."

"Bingo."

"See, Bingo had got out of the promo business while the getting out was good, before he got caught with his finger up a deejay's ass. Just like how he got out of the real estate biz. But when he jumped back into the promo gig, he wasn't hip to the new, '80s way of doing things, and his good old boy approach stuck out like a sore thumb. They nailed him with the help of this deejay in San Antone who had IRS problems and offered to cooperate. He wore a wire and let 'em videotape Bingo personally handing him five grand in cash to play the shit out of a couple of new records. They say he's a little paranoid about Bingo. I heard he wants to go into the witness protection program, and that's one of the things that has slowed up the indictment. But the word is the case is solid, and Bingo's looking at doing a dime in the pen."

"Hmmm."

"Hmmm is right. No major label is gonna do any business with a guy like me who used to do business with Bingo Torres."

"It would look bad."

"Look pretty bad. Yeah, you right, it'd look pretty bad, especially now."

"Well, Vick, there's no such thing as a good time to be blackmailed. But what could Retha Thomas have had to do with it?"

"Hell, I don't know, Martin. Maybe nothing. Maybe she was keeping an eye on me for the blackmail crew. That's the only thing that makes sense to me. Otherwise, I got no real enemies. I'm just here on the fringe of the music community, a junk collector, an average guy, 'cept maybe a little bit fatter than everybody else. I try to help people, make sure a guy can get the right kind of clothes to wear on stage, so he doesn't have to go to the mall and buy a bunch of trendy shit makes him look like an MTV clone. Make sure a guitar player has a decent, American guitar on stage. Tube amplifiers. Leather jackets. These goddamn records. I'm just an old fat rock and roller, Martin. I collect junk, and people come here looking for treasure, they think they found it. Who'd wanna fuck with me?"

"I give up."

"Come on, Martin. You want a guitar, a bass guitar? Come

on, what you want? I got a cherry '63 P-bass suit you fine. Ampeg scroll top, even an old Kay upright Willie Dixon played down at Antone's one time. Could let you have that for a C-note, you help me out. I gave Stevie Ray Vaughan that pink Strat of his. Gave the Thunderbirds all matching white dinner jackets one time. I help you, you want it. You gonna help me?"

"Help you what?"

"Help me handle this, you know. What can I do? I can't stand this kinda stress. I talked to my doctor yesterday, he said, 'Vick, you weigh three hundred and twenty pounds. You either gonna have a heart attack or blow up. My nurse has twenty bucks says you gonna blow up.' How do you like that? My goddamn doctor is laying odds I'm gonna have a heart attack."

"What about the nurse?"

"Fuck the nurse. I know I'm not gonna blow up. But I can't stand this stress. I can't make the payoff, meet some scary-ass guys on a country road in the middle of the night. I don't want my doctor to get that twenty bucks. I don't. Whaddya say?"

"Go on a diet. Try oat bran."

"Come on, man."

"It's not my problem. I don't need the stress any more than you do. I just got off the road and I'm trying to reassemble my love life. Getting involved with this isn't going to help that any. But mostly, I don't trust you."

I got up to leave. He looked disappointed. Sweat poured off his forehead and plastered one of the curly strands of hair to an area just to the side of his right eye, suggesting a deep gash in his head. He made a fist and ground it into the table.

"I wish I had some money to offer you, Martin. I don't have more'n fifty bucks petty cash. Business been slow. I could give you a thousand bucks after I get the record money, should be some time next week. Whaddya say?"

"We've all got problems. I don't need yours."

"All right, fine, Martin," he drawled, a big pout on his face. He stubbed out his cigarette and blew a cloud of smoke over me as I got up. "You're no more'n a little fixture in this town, you know, and you ain't gonna get no bigger."

"You've got better things to do than try to hurt me."

"I don't fucking need to, man. You're just a goddamn bass player, rehashing the same shit every night with a bunch of white boys trying to do something black people do a helluva lot better." He grinned. "Ain't the only thing they do better, what I hear."

I felt my neck stiffen as his grin widened.

"Say, how was that black pussy, anyway?"

His head rocked back like a bowling pin when I slugged him.

The next morning I went back to work at the collection agency. I didn't want to, but we'd been stiffed by the last couple of clubs on the tour and the money from Sunday night's gig had to go toward road debts. I had thirty-nine dollars in my wallet and a lot of dirty laundry. Welcome home. There was the Antone's gig this weekend and I had some money in the bank, plus I was expecting a royalty check from a song I'd co-written that was going to be a B-side of a single coming out on CBS in a couple of months. But a little running around cash would help, and with the resources at the collection agency I might be able to find out a little more about Retha Thomas and also Vick Travis, if I was so inclined.

Lone Star Detectives and Collection Agency had moved into a little rectangular building that used to be a Mexican restaurant just down South 1st from my apartment. The detectives operated out of a small building just in back that was formerly a tortilla factory. The two buildings were now connected by a narrow corridor that doubled as a break room. I could smell the coffee burning in the bottom of the urn as I sat at the desk in my cubbyhole, trying to readjust. It was hard.

I'd ridden, driven, and slept beside over eighteen weeks of highway, seen cars go off mountaintops, marriages break up, club owners go into DTs, flattened rodents broiling on the blacktop. There had been two or three governments overthrown, four US diplomats kidnapped or shot or both, a half dozen Texas savings and loans gone under, a number of wildlife species declared irrevocably extinct. But the office was the same. There was still an office fat girl pushing doughnuts and brownies to everyone who passed her desk, a bosomy redheaded divorcée who regularly teased me about accompanying her on one of her bimonthly Vegas junkets, a trailer house redneck who went to church every Sunday and K-Mart every Saturday, a couple of yuppie-wannabes who worshipped the Beatles, subscribed to *Architectural Digest,* and yearned for Volvos.

"It's good to have you back," said Jack Green, the office supervisor. "I guess you know what to do."

"Sure."

"We got a new computer system. You notice?"

I shook my head. He did a poor job of hiding his disappointment. Just like the time I hadn't jumped up and down over his decision to name his first-born son Dylan. "What can we expect from you, Martin? About twenty hours a week?"

"I think I can manage that. I've got a few things still up in the air since I got back, but . . ."

"We've got an office softball game and picnic on Sunday. We've been doing it every other week. Like to see you there."

"I don't know."

"You don't have to bring a glove, we've got plenty. But bring a covered dish, or, well, you probably don't cook, do you? How about some Doritos?"

"I promise not to come without any."

He nodded, adjusting a paisley tie on a cheap dress shirt. "How was the tour? Did you rock out, Martin? Lotta groupies following you around?"

"You know how it is," I drawled through a conspiratorial one-sided grin. You can't let people like that down.

He chuckled, squeezing his eyes shut, playing a wild lick on an air guitar, saying, "Yeah, man. You gotta take me along next time. I'll be your road manager, OK?"

"No problem."

He left me alone. I looked down at the stacks of files and envelopes marked "return to sender" and the late notices and all the sneaky city directories and microfiches full of names and addresses that were supposed to help me find people so the collection agents could call them and badger them into paying their bills. I felt like the new animal in the zoo and all the junk on my desk was some kind of new zoo food that the keepers were waiting for me to eat and say, Yeah, tastes great, just like the stuff in the jungle. It was going to be rougher than I thought.

I did some legitimate work, sorting out accounts, calling up some landlords and getting the names of relatives of tenants who'd skipped out. Because if they skipped out on their cable TV bills or their telephone bills, which we handled, there was a good possibility that they'd also done something to make their landlord want to fink on them. But I also fired up the computer that was hooked into the central computer at the retail merchants' credit bureau and pulled a credit file on Victor Angelo Travis. Just as I'd thought, he was pretty much of a cash operator, but he had taken out a small bank loan back in 1985. I called the bank. He'd put up his store for collateral, and at that time the store was worth a net of about $15,000. Then I entered the name of Retha Ann Thomas and the city of Los Angeles. A file came up. It listed her as unemployed, with Tower Records being her last employer. There were a few department store accounts, American Express, and the name of her bank. There was something a little disturbing about the waxy computer paper with the squiggly computer fonts, coldly revealing what it knew about her. I tore the printout off the printer, folded it, and slipped it in my jacket.

I looked around. I was probably the only guy in the room who knew the real words to "Louie Louie." It was 3:30, time for an afternoon break. Most of the other employees headed for the break room for some microwave popcorn, burnt coffee, or a diet drink. I went over to the front door, where Detective Sergeant Jim Lasko of the Austin police department's homicide division stood resetting his beeper.

"Howdy," I said.

"Howdy doo," he said. "You're under arrest."

"Man you have no sense of humor whatsoever," drawled Lasko as we rode toward downtown in his pickup truck. "None what-all."

"Put yourself in my shoes, why don't you."

With the thermometer registering somewhere between the high seventies and mid-eighties it was temperate for a May afternoon, the kind of weather that was pretty livable as long as you were under some shade. The windows were rolled down and the humid air and traffic sounds rushed through the cab, making our voices sound thin and raspy.

"I mean, I could arrest you if you didn't want to come down, but I don't have to. Do I?"

"Must be nice to have so many options. So what's the big deal if I skin my knuckles on Vick Travis's teeth?"

"Some people like to be punched out, some people don't. Some people don't so bad they swear out a complaint against you. They do that, we're supposed to respond."

"I thought that was for the robbery and assault division. Last I heard, you're in homicide."

"That I am, Martin, that I am," he drawled. He pulled his sunglasses down on his nose so I could see his eyes.

"All right, then, what's it all about?"

"I told you that the stuff we got from the lab didn't completely clear you any more than the circumstantial evidence we had would indict you. Didn't I?" I acknowledged that, yes, he had told me that. "So you just kinda went from one state of suspension to another. The thing is, you're still pretty high on our list of people to touch base with on the Retha Thomas thing.

Now we got some more chitchat to do. You know Donald Rollins?"

"He used to tend bar over at Steamboat, didn't he?"

Lasko nodded. "Made a damn good margarita."

"He's a hype, right?"

"Yep. They had to let him go when they found out he'd made a spare key for the Space Invaders machine and all the quarters were going in his arm."

"I seem to recall something about that. He borrowed one of Leo's guitars. It turned up in a pawn shop in Houston and Leo had to pay a hundred bucks to get it back since he didn't have any proof of ownership."

Lasko made a clucking sound. "Well, that's too bad. They found Donald tangled up in the duckweed over close to Marshall Ford Dam this morning."

"OD?"

He shrugged. "Hard to tell right off. A day or two in that lake water kinda complicates things. One thing we can tell, though."

"What's that?"

"He'd been beaten. Lacerations like what comes from being flogged with a whip or a belt. Handcuff marks."

"Weird."

"Yeah. It's a weird world, Martin. Know anything?"

"Why would I?"

"His sister claims that he was going down to pay Vick a little visit, last she saw him. That was Sunday, but somebody else claims they saw him down there Monday night, too. Way the time works out, it looks like it was about an hour before closing time, maybe not long before you dropped in on the place."

I thought about that for a second. "He drive a green Plymouth?"

"Yep. It was parked over by the dam."

"He left when I got there. I didn't even see him."

"Too busy assaulting Vick?"

"Aw come on, Lasko. That's my business. Maybe it was a mistake, but—"

"Damn right it was a mistake, Martin. What the hell were you trying to do, beat a confession out of him? I'm the law around here. You get a bug up your ass next time, come to me. It's my job to solve crime, it's yours to entertain people. Some day you fly off the handle like that you'll find that you've blown any chance you had of making it. The music scene needs you. APD don't."

"Oh, yeah. You're doing just fine."

"Yeah? Well which one of us is doing better? I don't see you on MTV. This is complicated and fucked up enough without having to deal with your bullshit. You punching out Vick is just the kind of thing that keeps you in the lineup. The Lieutenant . . . Well, forget it. You want a ride back?"

"What? Is that it?"

"Yeah, I guess so, for now. I told Vick, why didn't he just cool off for a bit before he makes a final decision on pressing charges. I suggest you go over and apologize to the big porker. But don't call him that."

"I won't," I said. "No use slandering the pigs of the world. When can I get my bass back?"

"Might be a long time," he said. "Retha Thomas hasn't gotten any better."

I went back to my apartment, fed the cat, and flopped on the bed so I could think about the situation. But I hadn't slept worth a damn in several days and ended up dozing off.

I woke up drenched in the proverbial sweat. The whole bed was wet. But it wasn't sweat. It was blood. The bed was stabbed with so many knives it looked like a pincushion, a graveyard for knifemen. Damn, what happened, I thought. I scratched my eyes out and threw them against the wall. Why wasn't I buried, too? Wasn't I sharp enough? Just because I had one little blackout. From far away, a church bell rang. But it sounded tinny. Even the Christians were cutting back.

The phone was ringing.

I shot off the bed like a man shot from a gun. It was Billy. He wanted to know, was I coming to rehearsal or not?

We had the lease on an old warehouse behind a pool hall owned by Willie Nelson on South Congress. It was about as ugly as things like that can be—corrugated tin on the outside, concrete floor and walls that had been sprayed with acoustic damping material that looked like petrified vomit inside. Leo stumbled in an hour late, smelling like a bar rag, and Ray never showed up at all. Nick and Steve had another gig to work, but they rarely worked rehearsals anyway. At least I'd remembered to bring the Danelectro bass.

We ran over a few songs we hadn't played in a while—"Nutbush City Limits," "Born Under a Bad Sign," and "Chain of Fools"—then took a break. Leo cracked open another six-pack and lit a cigarette he'd bummed from me. He didn't understand why I should have a pack if I wasn't going to smoke them.

"You about out from under this thing yet, Martin?" asked Billy.

"In a way," I said.

"I was just wondering, you know, for your sake," he said. "Anything I can do?"

"No, don't worry about it."

"Because people are starting to talk," he said.

Leo looked up. He was holding the cigarette in the hand in the cast, cradling that hand with the other. It almost looked like he was petting a smoking rabbit. "Only six weeks of this thing, guys," he said. "It's like playing guitar with a goddamn boulder on the end of my arm."

I sighed. Billy sighed. "What are we doing here?" he said. "Haven't we seen enough of each other?"

"I thought we decided to get together and work up some new songs," said Leo.

"Yeah. Whose idea was that?" said Billy.

"Ray's," I said.

We observed a moment of silent annoyance dedicated to the saxophonist.

"He sure seemed pissed at you yesterday, Leo," I said. "You know why?"

He shrugged, a dumb, innocent look on his face.

"Leo," I said, "why don't we go for a walk?"

He curled his lip at me. "Walk?"

"You know, you stand up, move your feet . . ."

"Something wrong with your car?"

"No," I said. "We could get some fresh air and talk."

"Talk?"

"Yeah, talk. Maybe you could tell me what's been eating you."

He cleared his throat and spit on the floor. "Well, look everybody, it's Martin Fender, the great bandleader. He walks, he talks, he takes his guitar player out on a leash. You wanna fire me, Martin, is that it? You got some other player in mind? Somebody who reminds you more of the late, great KC? Lemme tell you something, Martin, I can't drink as much bourbon as he could and maybe I don't play as fucking loud as he did, but I can play as good as him any night of the week and I didn't let my old lady get the best of me and then blow my fucking brains out."

I didn't say anything. Then, as suddenly as his hostility erupted, it faded, and his face fell into a slack, boyish expression. "Aw hell. I'm sorry."

"It's OK," I said, sighing. "Why don't we call it a night?" Billy nodded in agreement.

Leo said, "Well, you guys go on and go. I think I'll stick around, work on this guitar. Maybe sleep here, I dunno."

"Trouble at home?" I said.

Nodding slowly, he said, "Nadine, she . . . well, I think we need some, uh, you know . . ."

"Space," I said.

"Yeah, that's it."

I went over and slapped him on the back, then packed up my instrument. Billy got his sticks and followed me out. Once we were outside the warehouse, he said, "Don't worry, Martin. He's not as dumb as he acts. He'll work it out."

"Without our help, right?"

Billy sighed. "What can you do? Don't tell me you've never had a problem you didn't want to share with your pals."

"He's at the point where he's sharing it with us whether he wants to or not. We may not be the Three Musketeers, but sooner or later he's going to mess up bad, and we'll either be his accomplices or his victims. The world is not made up of a bunch of separate, insulated compartments, you know."

"OK, Martin. Whatever you say. But I'm no psychologist. I'm just a drummer. And right now, I've got a date with a girl around the corner from you who drives a Porsche. You think it would be OK if I park the van at your place and pick it up later?"

"Sure you don't want to use the van?" I asked.

"Nah, she's not the back of the van type," he said, laughing. "Neither am I. I got a bad back, you know."

While we waited for his date to pick him up, Billy and I talked about Donald Rollins.

"I wonder how a person gets like that," he said, "so *out there,* so cut off from everybody that they can just drop off the face of the earth? I mean, you gotta let a lot of things go to get like that, so that you just don't give a damn."

"And no one gives a damn about you," I added.

"Well, you're right there. I mean, we all liked him fine when he was tending bar, sliding those free drinks over to us, didn't we? I mean, he was a great guy back then, always on the guest list, we gave him free records and all that. But when he was rolling through the supermarket parking lots, asking people if they were 'looking for a bargain on some stereo equipment,' we didn't talk to him too much, did we?"

"He wasn't such a great guy at that point. Maybe he never was a great guy. Just because we might have been a little over-solicitous when he was living the straight life doesn't mean we out and out turned our backs on him when he wasn't."

"You're right. I'm just playing devil's advocate here. Besides," he added dryly, "he had Vick and Ed for friends, didn't he?"

"You mean, with friends like that . . ."

"I don't know much about it, man. Nothing, in fact. But I ran into Donald's sister this afternoon, and she was running them down pretty bad. Said they ruined Donald. Ruined him as a person."

A Porsche Speedster roared up, and Billy got up and shook my hand firmly. "What the hell, Martin? We all gotta go sometime." The Speedster's door swung open and I caught a glimpse of long, wavy blond hair. Billy climbed in, shut the door, and hollered out the open window, "Don't worry about it, man. Nothing you could do about it." Then they roared off.

I was sitting in the van, thinking that Billy was right. There was nothing I could have done about it. Donald Rollins had just been one of those people you don't know, but see often enough to pretend you do. It doesn't mean you're friends, and it doesn't mean you have any special obligations to look after him. But I'd snapped at Billy just a half hour earlier, saying that the world wasn't broken up into separate, insulated compartments. And he wasn't going to let me forget about it. I felt like a hypocrite.

I felt a disquieting mixture of familiarity and alienation sitting in the van. There was the stale smell of cigarettes and booze and road food and the characteristic scent of band equipment that has been given a good workout and then loaded into close quarters, and I knew that if I leaned back into the seat and closed my eyes the comforting sensation of rolling down a highway en route to another one-nighter would come easy. It struck me that the road trip had been, in some ways, like a working vacation. Now I felt a million little responsibilities tugging at me that I hadn't felt on the road. It was time to start dealing with them. I got out of the van and locked it up. Number one on my list of things to do was to pay Vick Travis another visit.

But before I did that, I went inside and drew up a little contract.

———

"I think you just might be crazy, Martin," said Vick. He held the typewritten pages under the light, waving them so that they crackled. "You want a shot of Cuervo?"

I declined, but he turned around and opened a drawer on the desk and brought out a quart bottle anyway. Then he made a face after he checked the level. "Damn. That Eddie's been in here again."

"Pushing a mop can make you work up a thirst real quick, I imagine," I said.

"So can blackmail. Sure you don't want a shot?"

"Not right now. What do you think of the contract?"

He poured a couple of fingers of the gold tequila in a shot glass and took it all in one gulp and picked up the contract again, hissing through his teeth as the tequila did its stuff. "OK, Martin, so you want my store. The way I read this, I give you the store in return for your 'assistance in a private matter.' Hah. I like that wording."

"But you also have my word that I'll help you for the thousand bucks you offered, plus pretend this contract never existed, *unless,*" I emphasized, "it turns out that you've lied to me."

"Your *word.*"

"I'm taking you on faith, you can take me. Share the risk, in other words."

"This joint's only worth about ten grand after debts."

"Used to be worth fifteen."

He tilted his head back and let out a laugh. "OK, fifteen. Whatever. You know, the funny thing is, after I get the hundred grand, even if I shell out twenty on this blackmail thing, I'll still have eighty. So I was thinking about lamming outta here. Maybe buy a farm in Mexico. So hell, if you're interested in running the place . . ."

"I'm not. I already told you, it's just insurance, encouragement for you to be straight with me. One other thing, though, I need to know."

"What is it now?"

"Donald Rollins."

"Don," he said, shaking his head. "Poor ole Don. Used to be a damn good bartender. Had this German shepherd named Alamo. Got run over by a semi. His old lady run off the next day too. Poor ole Don. Used to be a good bartender."

"Yeah, I share your sympathy," I said. "Did you give him any while he was alive?"

Vick's head rocked back as if I'd slugged him again. "OK, Martin, look here. Don owed me some money, and we worked it out, OK? He used to borrow money from me all the time, and we always worked something out. I didn't sell him no heroin. He was fine when he left here."

"I guess I'll have to take your word on it. But you'd better not be lying to me."

"I ain't lying, OK? Christ, Martin, you think I'd shoot up one of my friends with smack and dump 'em in the river?"

"No, I guess I don't. That's all for now, then. You going to sign the contract?"

"You get off my ass for a minute I might," he said, sighing and shaking himself. He started to write his name, then looked up suddenly as if pricked by some private thought. "You know, none of this would be necessary if the goddamn guy from the record company would fly in here in the morning with a check. Then I could tell these guys to kiss my ass, tell the whole world I used to do business with Bingo Torres, South Texas Payola King, aka Danny Cortez. None of this would be necessary if the IMF boys would just get here and do the deal."

As I watched him put the pen down to the paper again, I wondered why he hadn't said that before. Suddenly he leaned back in the chair and giggled.

"Martin, you know how he got that name, Bingo?" I shook my head. He leaned forward, grinning. "His daughter. When she was little, he'd hold her on his lap and play a little game, looking for her tickle spots. Whenever she'd start giggling, he'd say 'Bingo.' So she used to call him that instead of Daddy. She hasn't been around here in twenty years I bet, but I like to think she still calls him that. Kinda brings him down to size, you know?"

"Are you gonna sign that or not?"

He nodded and scratched out his name. "The kid wasn't more'n two, three years old when the wife took off with her. Mrs. Torres was a good-lookin' gal, too. Tall, blonde, looked kinda like Kim Basinger . . ."

He signed both copies, and he poured two more shots. After we'd downed them he looked at me with glassy eyes and said, "OK, now what? They called again today. They said to get the money."

"Where are you going to get it?"

For a moment, he didn't seem to have heard me. He got a faraway look in his eyes and said, "He's too good for me now. You think he cares about my problem? And it's his fault. But he doesn't care. He's too big, too rich to care."

"So what?" I groaned. "Where are you going to get the money?"

He laughed like a *bandido*. "You're gonna like this: from Bingo Torres."

The next morning I drove out there. Vick was pretty certain that Bingo was the right place to go for the money. For one thing, he'd have it. For another, this was the in-between world of pimping, smuggling, payola, land flipping, and other shady enterprises; honor and codes were more important here than the United Nations charter was among heads of state. But Vick didn't say all these things. He just rubbed his fat stomach and said, "A favor's a favor."

Only, they hadn't spoken to each other in three years, and that was why I was driving out over the high wooded hills on Ranch Road 2222, resisting the sideways pull of the winding road, thinking about how Vick had reacted to Bingo's achievement of success like a spurned lover, like every dollar that Bingo accumulated was another act of infidelity. It didn't matter that they hadn't been partners in Bingo's most successful ventures, it only mattered that Bingo had a huge house overlooking Lake LBJ and several black cars, including at least one Mercedes, while Vick Travis was still a junk salesman.

It was a blindingly hot morning with the convertible top down, the air clear but heavy with the smell of the ubiquitous cedar, and as I savored the road's swings to the left and right, it seemed that the situation had its own goofy symmetry. Vick and Bingo needed each other. Vick needed Bingo's money. Bingo needed to keep Vick off the stand if and when he went to trial. It didn't matter that, aside from the minor local records that Bingo had financed, most of Vick's firsthand information on Bingo's payola machinery was probably twenty-year-old news. I knew I wouldn't want him testifying at my trial—on either side. The jury wouldn't even hear his testimony; probably they'd just look at the 320-pound monster and say, Whoa, crime *is* ugly, ain't it? I briefly considered the possibility that Bingo was blackmailing Vick himself, just as a test of loyalty.

But Vick wouldn't be likely to incriminate himself and thereby risk having the IMF deal blow up in his face. Besides, in Vick's opinion, Bingo was too busy with his own legal problems to know anything about the IMF deal. However, someone knew. Someone who knew that Vick had something to hide.

The theory of the loyalty-test-blackmail scheme seemed to collapse under its own weight, raising more questions than it answered, and it fell apart completely when I heard the mellifluous Spanish-inflected tenor on the telephone, saying, Sure, come on out, I'm sure I can be of some help to poor Victor.

But I still wanted to ask him if he knew Retha Thomas.

The house was just off the road, high up on a scenic overlook, precariously situated just before a curve that dropped sharply down toward the lake. The place screamed for attention with matching turrets jutting up from the second-floor balcony, Texas flags waving in the breeze, but to take a good look at it while driving by was to risk going off the side of the mountain or colliding with an oncoming car.

I parked next to a black Mercedes station wagon, walked up to the front door, and rang the bell. A Mexican boy in huaraches and white shirt and shorts greeted me, let me in, and escorted me out back, all without speaking any English.

Three Hispanic men sat poolside drinking Big Red sodas as they watched an androgynous-looking teenage girl dive off the diving board. All three wore sunglasses, and all three giggled like school kids as the girl hit the water and they were showered with the spray.

The one in the middle wearing a black cowboy hat and a white *guayabera* put his Big Red down on the wrought-iron table, smiled, and extended his hand.

"Hey Martin," he said as he pumped my hand, "how's it going?" He pointed to a chair across from him, and before I got a chance to answer, added, "You know, you're a helluva bass player. Damn good."

"Thanks, Mr. Torres."

"Bingo, Martin, Bingo. Everybody calls me Bingo that I like. I don't like somebody, I send Roberto here to shoot them, right, Roberto?"

Roberto nodded, a stone-faced caricature of a Mexican gangster with an electric-blue suit and a black shirt, the collar open wide so you could see his turquoise necklace. The other companion looked vaguely like a professional man on holiday, a doctor or a lawyer. His suit was more conservative, his smile more tentative, his Rolex half hidden by a five-button cuff. He remained nameless.

"Martin, who was that guy, played a black Les Paul, left-handed, upside down?" he said, still smiling, scratching the back of his neck.

"Spider Wilcox?"

"Yeah, that's the one. You played with him back in '79, didn't you? Down in Harlingen, big rock festival?"

"Yeah, I played with him."

"That was a good show, Martin. You guys rocked their socks off, man."

"Thanks."

"You're welcome. I promoted that show. I made ten thousand dollars. Thank *you*."

"You're welcome," I said. "So you understand why I'm here?"

"You said that poor Victor is being blackmailed, because of me?"

"I'm afraid so. Because of Danny Cortez, actually."

He laughed, looked at his companions, who were looking slightly uncomfortable, and not because of the heat, and then looked back at me, and wasn't smiling anymore. "Don't mention that name again, Martin. OK?"

"OK." Evidently Bingo Torres, as Danny Cortez, had done some things besides act as executive producer and sing "It's a Man's, Man's, Man's World" in Spanish. Things that the feds would probably like to add to their indictment.

"So how come poor Victor needs this twenty thousand dollars? On the phone you said he wanted to *borrow* the money. That is what you meant, isn't it?"

"Yeah. That's what I said. He can pay it back real soon. It would be a very short-term loan."

He nodded. "That's good, because I have to wonder something. On the phone you say he needs the money because someone wants to go into business with him, but someone else wants to tell this prospective partner that poor Vick used to be partners with me. Am I right so far?"

"Yes, Bingo."

"You can't tell me who this person or persons are that want to go into business with him, but you say they would not go into business with him if they knew he used to associate with me."

"That's right."

"You know how that makes me feel? You know it hurts my feelings?" It wasn't something I'd considered, but I nodded sympathetically, just the same. He leaned forward. "Whenever I get a feeling, Martin, you know what I ask myself? I ask myself, Is this feeling just a sign of weakness, the voice of a demon or malevolent ghost of one of my family's past enemies, come to distract me? So I ask myself in this matter, Are my feelings really hurt, or is it a sign? A sign that someone is trying to *fuck* with me. Are you trying to fuck with me, Martin?"

"I assure you, Bingo, that I'm not," I said.

"Vick isn't asking for twenty thousand in exchange for not talking to the feds about me, is he?"

"No. It's a personal business matter, as I described."

He repeated the question, his voice a bit higher in pitch, but lower in volume, almost a soft whine. "Vick isn't asking me for twenty grand to keep his mouth shut?"

"No. That really isn't what this is about."

He sniffed, pushing his lower lip up under his upper so that it made a bulldog face. "No, Vick wouldn't ax me for money to keep his mouth shut because, *número uno,* he doesn't have the *cojones* for it, and *número dos,* if he wants me to help him keep quiet he knows I'll cut off his *dick* and shove it in his *mouth.*"

Roberto and the nameless one were like bookends. He didn't even have to defer to them for support. I had no one. So I was nervous when he said, "Have you ever been hang gliding, Martin?"

"No."

"This hill before us is a very good launching point. If you jump off here, you could sail for hours on the air currents, probably glide all the way to Lake Travis." He took a thoughtful sip of Big Red, smiled, and added, "If you had the sail. If you don't have the sail on your back, you jump off the cliff here, and you just die. Short ride. Very short ride." Bingo's cohorts stood like trained Dobermans, came over, and flanked me. Either *ride* or *die* must have been their attack word.

"Wait," I said, "I've got something to show you."

His eyebrows perked up. His soldiers eyed me cautiously as I reached inside my jacket and produced my contract with Vick. Bingo looked it over, then did some mental calculations and tossed the contract back at me.

Shaking his head, he said, "That shop isn't worth over ten, fifteen thousand. He's got big debts, you know. Maybe seventeen, eighteen tops, if he's still got some good guitars. But it wouldn't make sense even for a bumbling fatso to give it to you in exchange for extorting twenty thousand out of me."

"No, it wouldn't."

"Well, Martin, I hope you're not lying to me. And I hope that for your sake, Vick is serious about paying back the money soon. I already have a lawyer bleeding me to death."

"Yes, he's serious. I don't think he wants to stay in your debt a minute longer than possible."

"Poor Victor's new partner must be expecting things to get a whole lot better in the *ropa usada* market. Or did one of his little bands get a contract or something?"

"Tammy Lynn Johnson seems to be getting some play on the college charts," I said, looking for a reaction.

There wasn't. Not, at least, one that was visible. "I don't listen to college radio," he said. "Would you like a Big Red, Martin?"

"No, thanks. Are you going to be able to do it?"

"Oh sure, Martin. Sure. Glad to do old Victor a favor. Tell me, is he still over on East 1st Street?"

"Yeah."

"Does he still sleep there, upstairs?"

"I suppose so."

"Still fat?"

"Oh, yeah. Looks like he was poured into his clothes and forgot to say when."

The poolside scene jumped up and down in the lenses of his shades as he nodded, but the expression on his face did not change. "Lotta kids still hanging out at his store? Guitar pickers and guys like that?"

"Sometimes."

"What do you suppose they want out of Victor?"

"I don't know. I don't know if they know. Maybe they're hoping to pick up a name or get him to make a phone call, giving them a recommendation, or maybe they've got no other air-conditioned place to hang out for free. Vick *has* accidentally done a couple of people some good in the past, hasn't he?"

"Maybe so, Martin. Maybe so." He adjusted his hat, smiling, baring his teeth. "Are you sure you can handle this thing for Victor?"

"I don't see why not."

"You sure you don't want me to get somebody to take care of it for you?"

"Yeah, I'm sure."

"OK. I don't have the money here. Come back tonight. I'll have it. Make it eight, OK?"

"That's fine." I got up and we shook hands. "One more thing, Bingo—"

"What's that, amigo?"

"You wouldn't happen to have known a girl—"

"Retha Thomas?"

"Yeah. Know her?"

He shook his head. "No, Martin. Bingo can't help you there. I heard about it. Are they after you?"

"I don't think so," I said, trying to sound as confident as you can sound with an answer like that.

The three pairs of sunglasses were aimed up at me, then shifted away in tandem. The androgynous girl was back on the diving board. As I opened the back door and felt the rush of air-conditioned air colliding with the humidity and me, I heard the splash.

Then the giggles.

I stopped at a diner when I got back to town. I had ice tea, chicken-fried steak, and a newspaper. The headline story concerned a local state representative's fall from grace. He'd fathered an illegitimate child from a union with a girl in a massage parlor. His wife told reporters that he subscribed to several "pornographic magazines like *Penthouse*." He admitted that he had a drinking problem, joined AA and became born-again. He was forced out of office anyway. In the last three paragraphs of the story were certain details. One, he hadn't lived with his wife in over a year, and two, he'd been supporting the mother of the child since her second month of pregnancy. Three, he'd run unopposed in the last two elections. He was a dedicated liberal, a hard worker, and had an impressive congressional record. It seemed like just a few years ago the congressman's indiscretions would have earned him little more than a slap on the hand and a spate of bad jokes, but that was then and this was now and he was going back to Dripping Springs to raise chickens.

I flipped through the rest of the paper to see what else had changed since I'd been gone. But I couldn't concentrate.

I wondered why the South Texas Payola King wasn't aware that Tammy Lynn Johnson was catching on. You didn't have to listen to college radio, you could read about it in the trade magazines. Hell, you could hear about it in idle chatter down at the Continental Club. He didn't know about Tammy Lynn, but he'd heard about Retha Thomas. I did no better with this question than I did with reading the paper. I didn't even know why it should bother me.

I pushed around the remains of food on my plate and tried imagining the conversation I'd have with Ladonna if I called her now at work. Hello, darling, I'd say, Everything's OK now. I've gone to work for Vick Travis. He's being blackmailed, you see, because he used to be partners with the South Texas Payola King. South Texas is more popular than ever, but payola isn't. That's why he's being blackmailed. If his association with Bingo comes to light, he won't be able to sell his catalog to a major record label. Why am I helping Vick Travis, though? Because he's my only link to Retha Thomas. Retha came to Austin from Los Angeles and the only thing we know she did with her time here is go around to the local hip spots and ask questions about Vick. Vick has this thug who works for him who's been known to get violent with a weighted flashlight—you know, Ed the Head, the sometime bouncer at some of the clubs I play in. The Payola King is no peacenik, either. But I'm going to borrow twenty grand from him on Vick's behalf, in the hope that the blackmail thing is connected with Retha Thomas's coma. I feel obligated to her.

You and I both know I wouldn't have beaten her, and I'm pretty sure I didn't do anything with her that would truly hurt you. All right, I kissed her, and I may have gone back to her room with her. I don't know. I don't remember. I blacked out and I'm ashamed of it. Not because it was my fault, but because . . . I don't know what the *because* is. I'm just a guy who wanted to take in some bright lights and loud music on his first night back in town because my own gig didn't do it for me.

I knew I wasn't going to call Ladonna. The Ladonna of my imagination didn't like the things I was going to explain to her any more than the real one would. And the waitress was looking at me like I was on drugs.

And maybe I still was. It takes more than a day or two to flush a drugstore's worth of barbiturates and hypnotics out of your system. I still had a metallic taste in my mouth and sometimes, like now, my skin felt like it was on fire. Maybe a cigarette would help. I took out the pack I'd bought for Retha Thomas and rubbed it on my cheek, on my forehead, like an amulet.

I dropped one out of the pack and set fire to it, sucking the smoke down deep into my lungs. My lungs fought back, trying to kick the monkey. I coughed. The spasm hurt, like a rock thrown against my sternum. I inhaled again, blowing it out slow and even, letting it fan across the table, swirling around the sugar dispenser, colliding with the window glass, scrolling out in every direction.

Cars seemed to float by on the hot boulevard like boats. A centuries-old oak tree hugged the street corner, its knotty branches flowing out from its massive trunk like an upside-down lava flow, its massive mounding crown like a mushroom of green smoke. The poison felt natural, tingling nerves from toes to scalp, and I settled back in the booth, cozy, getting reacquainted with the demon.

The waitress looked good in her tight white skirt and black

apron, padding around the diner in white institutional shoes. She wasn't wearing hose, and her legs were firm and smooth and pale. The rest of her was firm, too, except for a slight roll around her waist that showed when she bent over to get hot bread out of the warmer. Her blond hair was double-braided in back, with a few fine strands wisping down around the nape. Her bra strap cut into her back as she reached up to clip another order on the wheel. I thought about that strap, cutting into her skin, and I thought about her skin. After sucking in another lungful of smoke I closed my eyes and thought about what kissing her would be like. Another kiss came to mind. It loomed large in my memory, like a traumatic blow, like a physical transaction. Not a kiss, but a promise.

"Would you like more tea?"

I said yes and watched only her hands as she refilled my glass with the pitcher. I stubbed out the cigarette and picked up the pack and stared at it. The camel looked sleepy-eyed and innocent, the palm trees and the pyramids and mosques looked classic, unchanging. On the side of the pack was a warning.

I put the pack away and tried to wash the cigarette taste out of my mouth. It was time to visit Retha Thomas.

# 11

Life still hung around her like a lazy aura, like a tourist who'd come to the River City and picked up some of the local bad habits, like indecision, tardiness, slow motion. The bank of machinery hooked up to her reminded me of a huge alien beast. The doctor cleared his throat.

"It'd be nice if she'd open her eyes and say howdy, wouldn't it?" he said.

I swallowed hard and nodded. I felt his gaze as I stepped up and touched her hand. Her skin was cold. I tried remembering her as hot and sweaty. The thought seemed inappropriate. Her body, encased in the white sheet and blanket, still showed off its curves, but now it was more of a thing, a thing whose functions had been farmed out to machines and tubes. It seemed like she needed a miracle, but her surroundings didn't smell or sound or feel like a place where miracles were made.

"Who was the girl with the spiky black hair who left when I got here?" I asked the doctor.

"Her name is Barbra. She's a good friend of Retha's."

Mr. and Mrs. Thomas were in the waiting room. He was tall and broad-shouldered with large, strong-looking hands, kind eyes, and salt-and-pepper hair. She came to about his chest, and her blue dress, like his dark suit, had the sad, deformed shape of clothes on people who'd been able to do nothing but sit, and pace, and wait. The doctor introduced us and excused himself. There were places to sit but we remained standing.

"The police say that you were the last person with her before she was attacked and beat up," Mrs. Thomas said abruptly.

Mr. Thomas coughed into his fist and glanced away. I got the feeling that this wasn't the way he would have started things off.

"That's true," I said. "I drank a drink that had been spiked. It was her drink."

"They told us that, too . . ." said Mr. Thomas.

"Who would want to do that to Retha?" she interrupted. "Why? What did she do to anybody?"

He put his arm around her and squeezed her shoulder. She broke away and sighed, massaging the back of her neck.

"I don't know," I said. "Maybe it was originally intended for me, but I don't think so. It could be that it was a random thing. It was a large party and this is a big city, not near as big as Los Angeles, but there are a lot of crazy people here. Someone could have made the drink for themselves and she ended up with it by accident, I don't know. I'd like to help."

"We live in Valencia," she said, "just thirty minutes out of Los Angeles. We know about parties and big cities and crazy people. Retha got her own place down in Hollywood when she left high school. She's got an apartment on a hill above the Capitol Records building."

"She'd been trying to get a job at a record company, and they kept jerking her around," said Mr. Thomas. "That's what I got out of it, anyway. She said they were calling her back and she was waiting for the right opening to come up, but it seemed to me they were jerking her around. I work for Lockheed, which you might think would be way different, but I've found that executives are pretty much the same wherever you are."

"So she just came out here for a break?" I said. "Did she know anyone in Austin?"

Mrs. Thomas answered that question. "Some of her friends had been talking it up. They said there was a lot going on here, a lot of opportunities in the music business. I think she thought that somebody here might have a job for her."

"Did she tell you who she'd been seeing here, where she might have gone for a job?" I asked.

They both shook their heads. "She really likes music," said Mrs. Thomas finally, her eyes downcast. "She thought she could do something with it."

"We always encouraged her in whatever she wanted to do," said Mr. Thomas. His voice was quiet, solemn. He seemed to be running out of steam. I was trying to find a way to say good-bye that wouldn't sound trite or unrealistically upbeat when I heard footsteps approaching, clattering on the tile until they reached the carpeted floor of the waiting room.

"Does somebody have a quarter so I can call Triple A?" It was the somewhat hoarse voice of a female. Bracelets jangled. "I locked my keys in the Mercedes."

I turned around. It was Retha's friend. Her hair was black with reddish highlights, with a daring, uneven cut that framed her heart-shaped face like a jagged helmet. Her complexion was light brown and flawless, but I couldn't figure out whether her features were Asian or Hispanic. Tall and swizzlestick thin, she wore a white sleeveless top and matching pants, a wide brown suede belt and matching boots. She had a white blazer draped over one arm, a leather carry-on bag hanging from the other, and jangling bracelets on the wrists of both. Her wide, sensual mouth was working over a wad of chewing gum.

"I thought you left fifteen minutes ago," said Mrs. Thomas.

"Well, I tried to," she said. She took off her wraparound shades and dug in her purse for something. As she rummaged through the bag one of the straps of her top dropped over her shoulder, and she had to twist herself around to get it back in place. I watched, fascinated, giving her the same berth a defensive driver gives a swerving, battle-scarred automobile.

"Barbra," said Mrs. Thomas, "this is Martin Fender. Martin, Barbra is a good friend of Retha's."

She gave up on the purse and gave me a wide-eyed look. Her eyes were red rimmed from crying, the irises a grayish blue, like a rainy sky. "You're that guy?" she said.

I nodded. "Maybe I can help you."

"Martin Fender?"

"Nice to meet you."

"Barbra Quiero. You have a coat hanger?"

I followed her out the hospital doors. A light breeze rushed past us from the parking lot, but the air felt dry and abrasive. Barbra pointed to a dark brown Mercedes fifty yards away.

"Was Retha visiting you here?" I asked.

"Oh, no," she said, her voice going up in pitch. "I know her from L.A. I flew in this morning, as soon as I heard. I'd like to find the psycho who tried to kill her."

"So would I. Let's get that coat hanger from my car. Is that a rental?"

"Nah. Belongs to someone I know." She blew a bubble the size and color of a ripe plum and popped it. There was a deep scrape down the side of the Mercedes. It looked fresh.

Luckily, she'd left a window rolled down an inch or so because of the heat and I was able to unhook the latch after just a few minutes. During that time, she explained to me that she had a small but airy one bedroom in Laurel Canyon on Wonderland Avenue. It was a guest house, and the owner was crazy for pink—pink walls, pink trim, pink tile. He even had two pink cars, an old Packard and a '59 Cadillac Eldorado. Geena Davis and Jeff Goldblum lived practically next door and so did that old movie star Lizabeth Scott. Did I remember her? She was the one who was like a Lauren Bacall substitute back in the '40s and '50s. I said I did. Barbra had been dating a club deejay for several months, she said, and she'd gotten to be friends with Retha during her frequent trips to Tower Records.

"I've got a few connections in the business, you know," she said, "and I tried to help her get a job after she left Tower. She really wanted a job at a record company. But you know, record companies don't really pay that well unless you're high up in the structure, and most of those jobs are held by men. And most of them are jerks."

"I know," I said. "I've had some experience with them. It's a pretty closed society."

She nodded. "All they'd offer her was an entry level position, even after all her experience as a buyer and assistant manager. She knew all the promotion guys really well and had even managed a couple of bands who were real popular on the LA scene, but all they offered her was what they call 'administrative assistant,' at two hundred dollars a week."

" 'Administrative assistant' is Los Angeles for 'secretary,' isn't it?"

She nodded.

"Maybe she found a job here."

"But she hadn't moved. She still had her apartment and phone, and you know, her *car* is still there. Why wouldn't she tell anybody?"

"I don't know. I'd still like to pursue the job angle. Maybe someone called her boss at Tower Records for a reference. Did she bring a lot of money out here?"

"I don't know."

"Was she getting her unemployment checks sent out here by someone?"

"How would I know? What are you getting at?"

"I'm just thinking out loud, I guess. I don't think they'd forward her unemployment checks out here. So if she had a friend or someone sending them out to her, then maybe they'd know what she was doing here."

"I wouldn't know. I didn't know any of her other friends. But I could make a couple of calls. I've got to do something, or I'll go crazy. You know?"

"I'm sorry."

"You'd like to help, right?"

"Yes."

"Good," she said, tight-lipped. The wraparound shades hid her eyes, but I felt their intensity. "Have you got any other ideas?"

"A couple. What gave her the idea to come out here?"

She shrugged. "People she's worked with, people in the business, me included, I suppose. There's a buzz about this town, with Stevie Ray Vaughan and Jimmie Vaughan and the Fabulous Thunderbirds and all your other bands that are hitting it big now. I guess she thought she'd have a better chance getting a job here than in LA."

"Did she ever mention anybody she knew here?"

She shook her head. "I didn't even know she planned to come out. I think it must have just been an impulse, you know. She was that way sometimes."

"Maybe so," I said. "I've got a couple of things I'm checking out. Maybe something will turn up."

"I sure as hell hope so." She adjusted her shades and said, "I'm staying at the Hyatt. Why don't you give me a call later?"

I said I would. She tossed her belongings in the back and got in. She cranked the ignition and turned up the air conditioner before closing the door. I noticed that she had fake fingernails. I wondered what the police had done with Retha's.

I went home and fed the cat.

I still had a few hours to kill before driving out to pick up the money from Bingo so I sprawled on the couch and kicked off my shoes. I watched the cat hungrily dispatch the bowl of pellets and thought about Retha's parents. They needed faith and reassurance. They wanted their daughter to recover, they wanted justice. More than anything, they needed resolution. Their daughter wasn't dead but she wasn't really alive, and they didn't know what the hell happened or why. But they didn't need to know everything I knew about the case.

I'd fed Barbra Quiero a few questions that I was interested

in, like how a girl living on unemployment managed paying for a couple of weeks at La Quinta and a rental car. I needed her help, if she had any to give, but I didn't tell her everything I knew about the case either. She seemed like the type who could complicate things in a hurry.

I poured myself a short drink and thought about other possible complications. Bingo's vague threat came to mind. He wanted to make sure I wasn't just hitting him up for hush money for Vick. That should be no problem, as long as Vick had been telling me the truth.

The cat jumped into my lap, digging in with his claws so all thirty pounds of him wouldn't slide off. He stayed on, but the Scotch glass shot out of my grasp and bounced across the floor, soaking the carpet. I thanked him by folding his ears back and rubbing his nose. Soon he was purring like a lawn mower's engine. I didn't need that drink anyway.

I called Ladonna, but she was in a meeting. I called the collection agency and told them I wouldn't be in. I called Ray and
he was cool and cordial as a gin martini and he said he'd see
me Saturday at Antone's, but that would be his last gig with
the band. I asked him why and he said ask Leo.

I called Leo's apartment but got a busy signal. After five
more tries I decided it must be off the hook. I called Vick and
told him I'd be picking up the money at eight. He said he knew
because Roberto, Bingo's right-hand man in the blue lamé suit,
had called him. He also said that the guys had called again and
said the payoff had to take place sometime in the next twenty-
four hours.

"So," he said, "however you wanna handle it . . ."

"Sure," I said. "I'll call you tonight." How *was* I going to
handle it? I didn't know. Because the payoff wasn't the goal
for me. My goal was to identify these guys, trace them somehow, and find out if there was some connection with Retha
Thomas. Maybe they'd know how she'd been paying her motel
bill. Maybe they'd know what she was doing in town. They
were interested in Vick, she was interested in Vick. Maybe they
didn't want the competition. If they weren't connected with

her, maybe Vick had decided that he was only going to pay one set of blackmailers.

If maybes were dollars, my last name would have been Trump. But for the time being, I'd have to settle for the maybes.

I popped a Willie Dixon tape in the Walkman and headed down South 1st Street in the Ghia. Deaf kids were bopping down the hill in front of the deaf school across from my apartment complex, signing furiously at each other. Joggers and cyclists were circling the hike and bike trail around Town Lake. The stylish new downtown high-rises huddled around the Capitol on the north side of the water, and the Hyatt crawled up from the southern banks. That was where Barbra Quiero was staying. It cost a lot more than La Quinta. I didn't give it much thought as I drove across the bridge. It was a nice day.

I needed to either patch things up between Ray and Leo or find a new saxophonist. I'd about had enough of Ray's high-hatting attitude anyway, and I was genuinely worried about Leo. If he was bound and determined to be a fuck-up, fine. He'd have all the company he wanted on the local music scene. But if he didn't straighten out soon, I'd have to look for another guitarist, too. And I didn't want to do that. Not now.

I picked up a couple of orders of flour tacos and guacamole chalupas at the Tamale House at 29th and Guadalupe, then drove over to Leo and Nadine's place just a few blocks farther up the Drag. The home-cooked Mexican food smelled so wholesome and satisfying, it seemed sure to help put things right.

But I could feel a sort of stale dread hanging in the air even as I knocked on their screen door. Leo was slumped forward on the couch, staring at the TV with the sound off, cigarette smoke curling up from the cast on his hand. I had to knock again before he came out of his dreary reverie and shuffled over to unlatch the screen.

The duplex was a wreck. Dishes were piled high in the sink in the kitchen and Leo's suitcases lay open in the living room with twisted pieces of clothing flowing out. And the dog wanted to go for a walk, badly.

"Shouldn't go out without a leash," said Leo, surly and languid. "Tying him up in the front yard would be cruel, and it's too hot to take him for a walk." He was in faded, frayed jeans and a dirty undershirt. Barefoot. He needed a shave and some industrial strength hair disentangler.

The dog's wagging tail was beating bruises on my calf. I petted him and put the bag down on the coffee table, unrolling the top to see if the aroma would do anything to lighten the gloom. "Hungry?" I said.

He raised his shoulders up so that his ears were even with them. "She might be, though."

"Nadine?"

A slight nod.

"Is she here?"

"In the back bedroom."

I picked up my groceries, walked down the hall lined with guitar cases, and knocked on the door. There was no sound. I pushed it open slowly.

She was sitting on the bed, facing the wall. At her side was a packed suitcase. Her waitress uniform was draped over a chair.

"Nadine . . ."

She jumped up and spun around to look at me with her wet eyes. Her hair was dyed an eggplant shade of black and cut in a trendy bob, but she was pretty in an earthy kind of way, not exotic, not tall. I knew that she liked animals, horror novels, and James Woods. Leo said she was a good cook, too, but they ended up ordering takeout a lot since she worked a lot of night shifts. Having grown up in a household with a working mother and four brothers, cooking for men had lost a bit of its glamour—for her, anyway.

"Oh heck, Martin. You startled me. I thought it was that worthless bastard."

"Want some tacos?"

She forced a smile, shaking her head. I'd lost interest in them myself. "What's going on, Martin?"

"I was hoping you could tell me."

"What does it look like?" She started folding a scarf.

"You two have been together a couple of years now. Isn't it something you could work out?"

She smoothed the scarf into the suitcase, saying, "Nope."

"Do you mind me asking what it is?"

She shook her head. "Nah, I don't mind, as long as you ask Leo. After all, he's in your band. You can look after him from now on." She paused, raising her eyebrows at me.

"What was it this time?" I said.

"Ask him."

"You know, Nadine, I'm getting tired of people telling me to ask Leo. Everybody's so upset with him, it must really be something bad. But before you make it all final, you might think about the good things you'll be missing—your home here, the dog . . ."

"Whoa, you got the wrong idea, Martin. I'm just going over to my mom's house to give Leo time to clear out. I like this house and I'm not giving it up. I hate to move more than anything, especially after I find a place I like."

"You're kicking him out, then."

"Uh-huh. But you're right about Frankenstein, I'll miss him. I hope fuckhead takes care of him."

"The poor pup really wants to go for a walk. I feel sorry for him."

She thought it over for a moment, then smiled slyly at me. "Yeah, the big black monster shouldn't have to stay cooped up in here all day just because Leo and I are at each other's throats. And I could use some fresh air too."

I followed her back through the house, watching as she glanced over at Leo a couple of times while she fastened the leash to the ecstatic Doberman's collar. Leo would look up at her but only when she wasn't looking at him. The dog hit the screen door as soon as it was unlatched, and the two of them lurched out with Nadine's arm straight out in front of her, the dog charging down the sidewalk, testing the leash, choking himself. I sat down on the other end of the sofa.

"What'd you do this time, Leo?"

He was holding the hand with the cast again. The cast was a little less startlingly white now, so it looked more like he was holding a slightly soiled white rabbit. He sighed and it seemed to take everything out of him. "Martin," he said, "I'm sorry, but I really don't wanna talk about it. I didn't hurt anybody but myself, OK?" He closed his eyes and chuckled quietly, saying, "It was one of those victimless crimes."

"You hurt Nadine. You call that victimless?"

"She's putting out her own kinda hurt, Martin. She hit me with a broom last night."

"You didn't hit her back, did you?"

"Nah. Let her have her fun."

"You know, I'm worried about you. I hate to butt in where it isn't any of my business, but you've got to admit you've been acting strange."

"At least I haven't had any blackouts. I *know* what I did Sunday night, even if I don't wanna talk about it."

"That's not fair, Leo."

He grunted and stared off into space. "Not fair, huh? Not fair . . ." He let the word trail off, as if it were a tendril of smoke waiting to be caught in a draft. "A lot of things aren't fair. We're living on top of a world of not fair. And *strange,* you wanna tell me what strange is, Martin? I don't know what strange is anymore. I just don't. From Fort Worth to LA, grammar school kids are toting Uzis and driving BMWs. Last night in San Antone some asshole was drinking with this old man behind a tire store and got pissed and beat the hell out of him, knocked both his eyes out with an ax handle and kept on stabbing him in the head with it. Afterwards he covered him up with tires, left him for dead, and went across the street to a bar and bought a beer. Parents are keeping their kids chained in basements, using them for punching bags."

He shook his head and sighed. "Everything's so damn depressing. I got kids stopping me on the street asking me for my autograph, telling me I'm cooler than Batman. When I get home, I got nothing but bills and an eviction notice. I know you got troubles too. Maybe you're just hassling me because it's easier than dealing with your own strange shit."

"You know that's not it."

"OK. But you got problems, I know that's a fact."

"And I know you and Nadine aren't having a typical lover's spat. Something real wrong is going on here. She's put up with jerks ever since she was born, and she puts up with them on the night shift, too. She wouldn't be kicking you out for something petty."

"You don't know that, man. She's a tough baby. She's so mean, she'd smash you in the face just to hear the bones crunch."

"You just said that to be funny."

His lip curled up in what might pass for a grin. I was almost glad he'd made the crack, as untrue as it was. "OK. Maybe I did. But maybe she's just not overjoyed to see her baby boy come back home. Maybe she's ready to start making breakfast for someone else because she thought she smelled eighteen weeks of pussy on my breath."

"Maybe. But I don't think so."

"OK. I'm a liar. But why don't you just let me root around in my own slop? Maybe I enjoy being miserable."

"Do you?"

"Naw," he said, sighing. "Hell, no. But I'm telling you, it ain't that big of a deal. I mean, it's over. What's done is done, and we'll either work it out or not. It doesn't have to concern you or anybody but me and Nadine."

"What if you told Nadine you were sorry and you really meant it? You think it's possible you could patch things up?"

He shrugged. "I don't know, Martin, she's really pissed. She's looking for a whole new baby boy here in these shoes. I don't wanna change too much, man. I don't wanna get a *job,* goddammit. I'm a guitar player, for chrissakes."

I jabbed him in the chest and said, "Leo, she doesn't want you to get a job. You were a guitar player when she met you. She just wants you to straighten up. When she gets back, tell her you're sorry. Tell her you'll start looking for a job so that if things don't pick up soon you'll have something to fall back on. You'll have a plan. Girls go for stuff like that. Plus, we're making a couple of hundred bucks each at Antone's on Saturday night. Sunday morning you go out and buy a cartful of groceries and Sunday night you take her out to dinner. What do you think?"

"I'll try it."

"Tell you what," I said, digging the band's American Express card out of my wallet and forcing it into his clenched hand, "take her out to dinner tonight."

"Thanks, man."

"Sure. You both need to get out of here for a while. Take her somewhere nice, but don't abuse it," I said, pointing at the card.

"You can trust me."

"I know," I said, pausing at the door, "because it wouldn't be a victimless crime."

Ladonna had to work late, but I caught her on the phone before I had to drive out to the lake again. I told her about Nadine and Leo.

"Maybe she just missed him when he was gone and hates his guts for it," she suggested.

"I think there's more to it than that," I said.

"Yeah, that's too simple, even for a romance between a musician and a nice girl."

"Spiky tonight, aren't we?"

"I'm sorry, Martin. I miss you."

"Well, don't run off with one of the realtors at the office just yet. I've got a feeling I'll be busy tonight, but I might be able to drop by."

"If that's the best you can do . . ."

"That's the best I can offer, Ladonna, unless promising *not* to come by would be better for you."

"Ouch. You didn't have to say that."

"Maybe it's the heat. I'll call you later."

"I hope so. Maybe we can start over then."

And that would have to do.

I drove out to Bingo's at eight p.m. and picked up the money in a silver Halliburton attaché case, and there was nothing to it.

At midnight we were sitting around in Vick's office. Vick drank tequila and sweated a lot. Every few minutes he'd put his hand up over his heart, as if to see if it was still there or still working.

Ed just sat there with a kitchen match between his teeth, looking menacing, knocking back slugs of Cuervo, glaring defiantly at the two of us as he did so. He bummed another one of Vick's cigarettes. Vick sighed, annoyed, then lit it for him.

"Don't you have a bouncer gig tonight, Eddie?" said Vick.

"Not tonight," he said.

"Why don't you go on home, then?"

"Not sleepy."

"Martin and I have something to discuss."

"Don't let me stop you."

*"Eddie . . ."*

"All right, all right." He left.

When we heard the front door being locked, Vick put his hand back on his heart, shook his head and said, "I guess I'll make it. Tell me something, is that a gun in your jacket?"

"Yep."

"What're you planning on doing with it?"

"It's for protection. Nine-millimeter Beretta with a fifteen-round clip."

He shook his head. "Guns scare me, man. I don't think you should be hauling that around."

"There have been times when I wished I'd been hauling it around, Vick. I don't intend for some asshole to get the better of me if a gun is all it would take to prevent it."

"Well, you don't really think you'll need it on the payoff, do you?"

"Probably not, the way I figure it. After all, it's not like a kidnapping payoff. It's just some unknown guys who want to bleed you. I don't think it's gonna be too scary."

He shuddered. "I'm still glad you're handling it. I don't wanna have a goddamn heart attack. All I want, get these guys off my back, then get the hundred grand. I got a feeling those IMF guys are coming to town tomorrow. They look over my contracts one more time, talk to the bands' lawyers, or whatever, and they write me a check."

"Too bad we can't put these guys off till tomorrow."

"I told you, man, when they called they said it had to be tonight."

The phone rang.

Vick jumped and turned red and I thought he was going to have a coronary right then. I answered the phone and a deep, gruff voice said, "This Fatso?"

"No. But I'll have to do."

"Who're you?"

"Martin Fender."

He grunted. It didn't sound like the grunt of a man who was easily impressed. "I heard of you. You handling this deal for Fatso?"

I grunted.

"You better have the money."

"I've got the money."

"OK. I don't give a fuck who brings it, long as they don't come with any silly ideas or any goddamn cops. Tell Fatso that."

"All right. I'd just like some assurance—"

"Fuck you up the assurance. You got an assurance that if

tonight doesn't make us 20K richer we make a call to the right guy on the left coast."

"OK."

"Behind Rosie's Roadhouse on Ben White Boulevard at two a.m. Don't fuck up."

After I hung up I said, "It sounded kind of like Ed the Head."

Vick shook his head, soaking up the sweat from his temples with the red bandana. "No way. Eddie loves me, man. Besides, he doesn't have a phone."

"It doesn't matter. He hasn't been gone more than two minutes. He wouldn't have had time to get home unless he was staying at the hotel next door. I just meant that he had the same kind of voice. Sort of generic local redneck. I didn't think it was him."

"Of course it wasn't."

"You do trust him, don't you?"

"Sure I do. What'd they say?"

"They want me to meet them behind Rosie's Roadhouse at two a.m."

"Well, this is it, then."

"Yeah. Maybe I'll leave now. I heard at the police station that Morganna was out there this week."

"She the girl with the giant tits, about sixty-five, seventy inches in the bust?"

"Something like that."

He grabbed his chest. "Oh, lord."


By the time I'd gotten there, Morganna had already done her thing. I bought a beer that cost more than a six-pack would, drank it, and got depressed. Anything you saw in the club, you could see reflected several times more on the mirrors that walled the place. And once should have been enough. Between the looks on the faces of the dancers, the looks on the faces of the customers, and the face of the bass player in the mirror behind the bar, it seemed that everyone in the room had come for some sort of grim task. I didn't feel any cheerier, however, waiting behind the club in the car after closing time.

You could smell the sour cocktails in the dumpster. You could smell the asphalt cooling in the night air. The muffled doom-doom-doom of a disco bass drum pulsed away inside, giving the clean-up crew a beat to work to. Stars winked overhead, cars whooshed down Ben White, my feet tapped out static beats. Where were those sonsofbitches?

When the music stopped there were three cars left in the back lot. A late model red Ford pickup coasted around the corner and stopped inches from my passenger side door. My hand went instinctively to the gun in my jacket. Because the Ghia sat so much lower than the pickup, I couldn't see the driver. A passenger got out and walked around to my window. He was a tanned body builder in tight new Wranglers, cowboy shirt, cowboy boots, and a white straw cowboy hat with the brim bent low in front. Amber marksman shades hid his eyes. He spat before he cocked his head at the driver so that I'd take note of the double-barreled shotgun snaking out of the pickup window.

"Let's have the money," he said.

I showed him the Beretta.

It was possible he'd seen one like it before. Or maybe he didn't know what it was. Maybe he thought it was a cigarette lighter. In any event, he wasn't impressed.

I said, "Why not let's have a big red hole in that cowboy shirt?"

"Bad idea. You do that, you get blown in half, we get the money, and Vick Travis's little secret gets told."

"This isn't the way I wanted it to go," I said.

"I don't remember negotiating with you, Fender. Just give me the money and you won't ever see or hear from us again."

"Is that a promise?"

"It's the truth. Now gimme that briefcase."

"Just one thing I'd like to know. Did you have anything to do with Retha Thomas?"

His face turned slack. "Nope, sure didn't. Sure as hell didn't, and I don't know who did."

His answer was so simple and easily given, I was ready to believe him. He'd even stopped pushing for the money. However, the shotgun made a clunking sound on the pickup door, meaning that expedience was still an issue.

"You've got no reason to lie to me, since you've got a pal with a shotgun, right?"

"I never beat up a woman in my life," he said.

"What about your pal there in the truck?"

He grinned. "Only woman he hated enough to kill was his wife. But she went and died of cancer. But that's none of yer bid-nizz. How about it?"

I gave him the briefcase.

He took it, said, "Thanks, pardner," and walked around the back of my car, stopped at the right rear tire, and jabbed it with something. "One more thing," he said, "don't be following us."

I felt the car start to list and heard the hiss as the air went out of the tire, and he got in the pickup and they drove slowly away, $20,000 richer. There was no license plate and no dealer's name engraved on the back bumper, so I just sat there feeling numb and ineffectual.

After a few minutes of that I got out and started changing the tire. I pried off the hubcap and started in on the lugs. Lying flat, the hubcap was shiny enough to reflect the streetlight behind me and a group of bats as they fluttered around it. Austin is home to the largest urban colony of bats in the world, and I appreciated the company. I also felt no threat from them. Less than one percent of bats contract rabies. Even vampire bats, who need only about a teaspoon of blood a night, are timid and rarely attack humans.

I was loosening the lug nuts when I heard footsteps at my back. Chills ran up my spine—I'd left the gun in my jacket, which I'd left in the car. A spiral of crayon colors swirled on the hubcap as the figure approached. I turned around.

It was Barbra Quiero. From my crouched position, she seemed taller than ever, and the streetlight immersed her in an eerie, bluish glow. Her lips seemed to be a strange shade of translucent, purplish red. "Need some help?" she said.

"No," I said. "What are you doing out here?"

"I've been parked out front. I knew I'd see you when you left, but I was starting to think you'd left with someone else."

"Why would it matter?"

"I'm onto you. I was over at La Quinta when I overheard the desk clerks talking about you. One of them said you came back to the motel with Retha. So I've been following you. You've been busy."

"You could say that." The lug wrench felt cold in my hands. So a motel clerk saw me accompany Retha back to her room. Was it possible? I didn't like the idea. I wondered if Lasko had heard this information.

"We need to talk."

"I know. Where do you want to go? I'm getting tired of the scenery here."

She ran her fingers through her hair. The jagged cut quickly sprang back to its former shape. "I feel stupid for suggesting it, in light of things, but why don't you follow me to my hotel?"

"All right," I said. "You can trust me."

"I hope so," she sighed, looking back over her shoulder. "I think some guys have been watching me."

From her seventh-floor window, Austin looked quiet and tidy. Town Lake looked like a shimmering Lurex sash laid across the city's midsection. I knew it wasn't as peaceful as it looked. The capricious currents below the surface swirled wickedly around the trees and flood debris that had been submerged when the river had been dammed. That lake ate people—swimmers, boaters, careless fishermen. I checked my watch and cursed myself, wishing I'd called Ladonna earlier. Calling her now would be awkward, since calling a nine-to-five person at four a.m. and telling them everything is OK is going to be awkward, no matter what. Calling Vick and telling him that the delivery had been made with almost no complications was easy. He sounded relieved. Ice clinked in glasses behind me. I looked up and saw the reflection of Retha Thomas's friend, sitting erect on the bed, filling two of the squat hotel glasses with gin and tonic. I thought of the drink as bitter medicine.

"I was trying to buy some information about your friend," I said. It wasn't exactly a lie.

*"Trying?"*

"Wimpy word, isn't it?"

She shook her head, her mouth turned down in a bitter curve. Her lips were still a rubbery purplish red, even out of the blue streetlight. "Tell me about it."

"No. I think Retha knew something that caused someone to try to kill her. I'd rather not tell you what I think it was. Not right now."

She turned away and drained her drink. I made us a couple more, determined to sip the next one and call it quits. "So who is this desk clerk?"

"A young nerd, probably his first job. Not too tall, blond hair, glasses. I think his name might be Bob."

I sipped my drink and listened to my heart pound. There had to be a mistake. With all those barbiturates in me, I didn't think I could have made it up to her room unless I'd been carried. And there would have been fingerprints that belonged to me. If there had been, I'd probably be in jail now, instead of where I was. I told her so.

She unwrapped a stick of gum and stuck it in her mouth, then tossed the pack in the general direction of the large hand-bag on the floor by the bed and crossed her legs. They were cigarette legs, long and slim.

"Are you sure about this desk clerk thing?" I repeated.

She leaned back and worked the gum over slowly. "Let's say it's true. Let's say it's a fact that you went back to her room. They say Retha didn't have intercourse before the attack. But that doesn't get you off the hook. Maybe you wanted to have sex with her but you were too messed up to get it up and you took it out on her."

"That's ridiculous."

"Is it? I don't know you. Maybe you turn into some kind of psychotic monster when you're high. Maybe Retha thought she had a real man with her but you turned out to be a nothing, a zero, a guy with a little shriveled peanut, a chicken dick. And you beat her up because you couldn't take it. Maybe—"

"All right, that's enough," I said. The coarse tirade was like a slap in the face. She'd surprised me, but that had clearly been her intention. "For one thing, she clawed the person who attacked her, a person with a different blood type than mine. Anyway, I *know* I didn't do it, and I think you're lying about the desk clerk. So what's the point of this?"

She stared, her skin smooth as polished wood, her grayish blue eyes impenetrable. She looked so hard and alien that it was difficult to be mad at her. "OK, I admit it, then," she said finally.

"Admit that there's no desk clerk?"

"Uh-huh."

"So what am I doing here?"

"You're here to prove how easy it is to get you to go back to a hotel room with a girl, that's what. I've been trying to figure out what kind of a guy you are."

"Oh for chrissakes. You follow me late at night and walk up and startle me, then use some bullshit line to get me up to your room so you can blast me with a bunch of locker room pseudo-Freudian bullshit. Man, you are strange. What's the verdict, anyway? Am I strange enough for *you?*"

She sneered defiantly. "Well, I guess I tricked you to get you here, but it sure wasn't hard. Maybe it's because you feel guilty and you still don't know exactly what you did that night. But you don't seem like the kind of guy to do that to Retha. I mean, you probably wouldn't get so upset you'd beat up a girl if you went back to her room and couldn't get it up."

"Well I'm flattered," I snapped. "Look, I know you're upset

about your friend and you wonder about me. I wonder about
me too, but not about whether I'm guilty or innocent. What I
need is constructive help, not little psycho-sexual mind games."

She blew a bubble, popped it, sucked it back in. It snapped
like little firecrackers as she chewed. "OK. I don't know what
I'm doing. If only she wasn't so helpless, it wouldn't be so bad.
But she is, and I can't get used to the idea that I'm not able to
do anything about it. In fact, it's driving me nuts. Retha was
the same way, restless. That's probably what put her on a plane
to Austin."

"How long did you two know each other?"

She shrugged. "We'd been friends a few months. Six, maybe.
Before that we kept seeing each other in the record store, like
I said before. One day I invited her to lunch, and we started
going to clubs together after that. It's not like we were old high
school chums or anything.

"She liked to go to this Thai restaurant on Vine in Hollywood,
right across from the Capitol Records tower. She always ordered everything extra hot and spicy. Retha was never satisfied
unless she broke out into a full sweat during her meal. Once I
told her that if she liked hot food and music so much, maybe
she should check out Austin. I was here a year ago, with a
band."

"You said you didn't know any of her other friends?"

"No, she's pretty much a loner. I mean, she was really out-
going at her job and everything, but she was always real in-
dependent, too, like she didn't really need anybody except her
parents and her boyfriend. She spent most weekends with her
parents. She had a boyfriend for quite a while, a year or so,
and they kept pretty much to themselves, you know. So after
they broke up, she didn't really know what to do with herself.
But it wasn't because she's shy. I just don't think she's the kind
of person who needs a lot of friends."

"Do you know this guy? I'd like to talk to him."

She shook her head. "Nah. He sounded like a real dork, too.
I don't think I'd wanna know him."

"What was his name?"

"She called him Bone. It's easy to remember, just think of 'bum.' That's what he was. No job, no apartment, not even a car. And in LA, that's really the lowest, next to being homeless, 'cause even a lot of them have cars. That's all I know."

"I almost think I should fly out to LA and ask around. Maybe I should just talk to her parents."

"They don't know anything. All they know is Lockheed and their little comfy suburban lifestyle. Hollywood and rock and roll might as well be another planet. You'd only upset them."

"You might be right. But still . . ."

"I talked to her boss at Tower, like you wanted. Nobody called him from here about her, or anywhere else, for that matter." She leaned back on the bed and kicked off her boots. "Got any other bright ideas?"

"Not a whole lot. Did you get a license number on the car you thought was following you?"

"No."

"What about the make?"

She shrugged. "They all look alike nowadays."

"But you're sure someone's following you, watching you?"

She nodded. Her eyes started to well up, and she didn't seem to know what to do with that big mouth, lips pressed together, rubbery and purplish red. "Maybe they wanna rape and kill me too."

The curtains were open, a gray moonlit sky out there coated with glass. The door was double locked, and the only sound besides our voices and the ice clinking in our glasses was the low muted hum of the air conditioner maintaining the coolness of everything, the air, the chair I sat in, the thick carpet beneath my feet. I looked at Barbra, rolled up into a ball, hugging herself, crying.

I glanced around the room. She was as messy as Leo. Clothes were everywhere. There was a portable CD player on the table by the window, with a dozen CDs scattered around. Gum wrappers, *People* magazine, perfume, makeup, panties. There was a bra trapped under a room service tray atop the TV, the strap dangling down in front of the screen. Curled up by my foot was a tiny zodiac scroll, the kind you find next to the breath mints at the Minit Mart. Back on the bed, she was a solid ball of confusion, a human knot.

I knelt down by the bed and touched her. She kept sobbing. The thin muscles of her back were clenched tight as braided cables. I put my arms around her and soon hers were locked around me, the fake nails digging into my back. Her tears made my face wet. I squeezed her harder, but it didn't do any good.

"Oh, man, why?" she cried, nibbling my face.

I pulled back a bit and said, "I'm sorry."

Close up, her face was a study in extremes. Her rain-colored eyes, so large and wet. Her mouth too wide, her lips too full. They quivered against her teeth. Her cheekbones stood out, especially next to the smallness of her chin. She reminded me of a cat: the closer you look, the deeper the mystery.

I got up and her arms dropped, her fingers clawing at the covers. "I *am* sorry," I said.

She didn't say anything. She just turned away and faced the wall.

I drank some of my drink, realized I didn't like it, realized the stupidity of drinking just because I was in a hotel room with a strange girl in a strange situation. I thought about Retha and her bloody nose as I wiped Barbra's tears from my face, and had to look down at my hands. It was only tears.

"Don't touch me anymore," she said. "It just messes things up in my mind."

"OK."

"You think I want to be here with a guy who may have murdered my friend?"

"You know I didn't."

She turned over again, to face me. Her face was flushed, her eyes swollen, but her hair was unmussed, still clumped into sharp, accusatory spikes. "No, probably not. You seem like a good person. But on the other hand, you're just a guy. Guys do weird shit, they hurt you and fuck around with you and then they get that innocent look on their faces, saying, Who, me? I've seen it so many times. They can do anything, any fucking thing, then put on that innocent act, like they've been doing since they were little boys, breaking the neighbor's windows with baseballs and stealing cookies out of cookie jars."

She sat up and rubbed her fists in her eyes. "No," she said, "I know you didn't do it. But the person who did it? I think you know him."

I lit a Camel and blew the smoke up toward the ceiling. I felt like a smoker again. Maybe I'd never quit. When I looked at her again, her eyes seemed to be looking through me. She probably didn't even know why she'd said what she said. She just did, and that was that. She reminded me of my cat, ripping the stuffing out of my couch, looking over at me, daring me to give one good reason not to do it, one that would mean something to a cat. We'd used up everything we'd come to the room with.

I told her that she should call me in the morning and to call the desk if she heard any noises outside her door.

As I drove home I felt completely exhausted, as if I'd been beat up. And I noticed something for the first time. Full moon.

I dreamed I was struggling with a furiously tangled guitar cord. The knots were insidious and vague, defying every probe of my clumsy fingers. I couldn't remember why I wanted to unknot the mess in the first place, but it occurred to me that it would be a good idea to find the other end of the cord. When I found it, it was in Barbra Quiero's hands. She said that the mess was all my fault. Then I woke up. It was a helluva way to start off the day.

It was noon. I got up, put water on to boil, ground some coffee beans, and fed the cat. His life was simple. No coffee, cigarettes, rhythm and blues. No car insurance, intraband soap operas, or two a.m. payoffs. A simple life, no answering machines. Mine was blinking five times. I rewound the tape, turned the volume back up, lit a cigarette, and finished making the coffee.

The first message was from Leo. He said he wanted to talk to me, that it was important. The second message was from Lasko, saying to give him a call when I got my lazy ass out of bed. I stopped the machine and dialed the homicide department. He wasn't in, so I left a message. I called Leo, but there was no answer.

The next two messages were from local rock writers. They

were both calling about "the, uh, Retha Thomas thing." I knew that the first writer—by his reputation and the tone in his voice—just wanted a juicy little story for his paper. The second one wanted to know if there was anything he could do to help. I thought it would be better all the way around if I didn't return either call.

The last message was from Vick. He was on his way to the bank, he said, to cash a $100,000 check from IMF Records. Why didn't I drop by later so we could square up? You could hear him burst into laughter as he hung up the phone. I poured a cup of coffee and sat down with the paper. Damn, it had really happened. I hadn't realized until then that the concept of the porkish thrift shop proprietor getting a hundred large from a major record label for his little indie records had seemed abstract, fictional. I suppose I felt a twinge of jealousy.

Or maybe it wasn't jealousy, exactly. I'd made the payoff for him and he got his hundred grand. What did I get out of it? Retha Thomas was still in a coma, and I didn't know who had put her there.

The coffee was good. I called the neighborhood florist and ordered some birds of paradise to be delivered to Ladonna at work. They said they'd probably get there in an hour. I'd wait, then call her. To kill time I got out the Danelectro bass and started plunking. Founded in 1948 by New York electronics buff Nathan Daniel, the Danelectro Corporation produced a line of guitars, basses, electric sitars, and other strange stringed instruments (in addition to amplifiers, one of which also served as a guitar case) that were not only incredibly innovative, but cheap. Danelectros were the VW Beetles of rock and roll hardware during the company's heyday between 1956 and 1968. Now they were collector's items. The pickups were sheathed in chrome lipstick tubes. The bodies were made of particle board and Formica. Streamline Moderne relics, they were as American as Buicks, Bowl-A-Rama, and Bob's Big Boy. Mine was a dual cutaway shorthorn model with copper sparkle finish. It was lightweight, had only fifteen frets, and would produce, after some coaxing, a tone that was at best scratchy and twangy, providing a perverse satisfaction similar to that of a cheap, marginally reliable sports car.

The strings sent vibrations through the body and made it seem alive. Normally that was a good feeling, but now it reminded me that someone had picked up my candy-apple red Fender and tried to beat the life out of a girl with it. Would it ever feel the same again? Would it be spattered with dried blood and smudged with fingerprint powder when the police gave it back to me? Would I even want to see the thing again?

It was weird. I felt violated, but feeling that way almost seemed like an infringement on the rights of the comatose girl. She was the one who'd really been violated. Violated to death, maybe. But I felt that way anyway.

Some part of my subconscious mind was still waging a small war with Barbra Quiero, too. In a way I understood her lashing out at me, testing me, sniping away at vulnerable spots. But on the other hand, I felt an old-fashioned ambivalence toward her. She was both attractive and repellent, clever and simple-minded. The world was full of people like that, and I didn't have to be her whipping boy.

There was a knock at the door. It was Lasko, his face damp from the heat as he walked in carrying a bass guitar case. He was dressed in a blue blazer that was a size or two too small and big brown box-toed shoes. The getup was as uncomfortable for me to look at as it must have been for him to wear. "Got any coffee left?" he asked, sitting down on the couch, tripping the latches on the case and taking out his own bass guitar, a sunburst Fender Precision. It was a good one. I'd found it for him in an East Side pawn shop.

"Sure. You in court today?"

"Yep."

"Then you only want half a cup, right?"

"Sure, that'll be fine," he said, distractedly plucking out some beginner's runs on the instrument.

I brought him the coffee and set it down on the coffee table.

He nodded a thank you, then reached down to the case and brought up a pint of Jack Daniel's. He poured a slug into the coffee, took a sip, and leaned back. "Got a couple hours' recess. I hope you got some time."

"Sure," I said, strapping my bass back on. "What'd you want to start with?"

We did a quick review of some songs I'd taught him during his last lesson—"Linda Lu," "Roadhouse Blues," and "The Thrill Is Gone." His technique was improving, and his timing was starting to get so good that I had to wonder if maybe he'd gone into the wrong profession. Timing is hard to practice unless you're doing it with a band, but if you don't work on it, once you do get with a band you're no good to them. So I was an insistent toe-tapper with Lasko, and he seemed to have a natural feel for not only keeping the beat, but also for playing around with it, teasing it, purposely coming in a bit late, anticipating it with a leading note. But he had questions.

"I wanna know why is it you can't tell me what the scales are," he said, slurping the coffee and whiskey, eyeing me across the cup suspiciously.

"You mean the major and minor scales?"

"No, you know what I mean. How some songs have these flatted thirds and sevenths, and some don't. How some songs have them both flatted and natural. I mean, you showed me these keys, and hardly any of these songs we've been learning follow them."

"Well, besides the major and minor, there are modes. There's the mixolydian mode, there's also what we call the blues scale, which we've been using a lot, especially in songs like 'Linda Lu.' " I tried to look smug and authoritative, but I could see by his hostile expression that it wasn't working.

"You mean I gotta learn a whole new scale or mode for every song?"

"No. Just listen to the guitar player and the basic melody, the chords. It's just the way it is. Sometimes you might have a half step instead of a whole step so you can lead into the next chord. Or, you might have your flatted sevenths happening when you're doing a walking bass pattern and you're descending down to the root note of the next chord."

He was shaking his head. "Goddamn, it just doesn't seem like there're any rules to this shit. How'm I supposed to learn how to do it if every time I learn something, I find out that that's not necessarily the way it is?"

"If you're just worried about memorizing the notes, we could get some little round stickers and stick them to the fretboard, and write the names of the notes on them."

"Fuck you."

"You've just got to be flexible, Lasko. Go with the flow."

That seemed to irritate him even more. He sighed and nodded, relaxing his grip on the bass. "Go with the flow, huh."

"Yeah, just think about the song, instead of the rules, think about—"

"I *know* what 'go with the flow' means, Martin."

I studied the wrinkles around his tired eyes, the pallor in his cheeks. "Not making your police work any easier, though. Is it?"

"No, it ain't. I been trying to go with the flow on this Retha Thomas thing, and so far, it ain't working. But we don't have a helluva lot to go on."

"Nothing at all?"

"Well, no. Not exactly. Actually, I wanted to tell you, we found out some more stuff you might be interested in, seeing as how you and Vick Travis are so buddy-buddy these days."

"What's that supposed to mean? You're the one suggested I go to him and apologize."

"I didn't mean you should move in with the guy," he said, making a face. "I've seen your car there two, three times this week now. But whatever, it's your goddamn business. What we found was that Donald Rollins evidently got a spike full of brown tar or china white and went for a walk and either jumped or fell in. I know it sounds suspicious, but the ground was all wet and there's only one set of footprints. We haven't got all the reports back from the lab, but some of the whip marks on his back were months old."

He paused and watched my reaction. I thought about what he said, but I just couldn't do anything with the information.

Lasko shrugged. "What can I say? I don't know what to make of it. But there's all kinda people out there, people like Donald Rollins, people who look for people like Donald Rollins. The X rays did reveal that he had a broken arm about a year ago. I thought you might be interested to know who paid the emergency room bill."

"This is what you wanted me to know about Vick?"

He nodded. "Probably doesn't mean anything."

But it did mean something. It didn't seem pertinent to Retha's case, but it put a darker shadow over Vick's way of "helping out" people in the music scene. Evidently Donald Rollins had been late in paying back one of Vick's loans, and a broken arm had been Vick's way of "working it out." Then he must have felt bad about it and paid the hospital bill. But Lasko didn't seem to know about that. He was still talking.

"Old Vick's been around forever, right?" he went on, and I couldn't tell whether he was being sarcastic or not. "Sorta fatherly type. I know two, three guitar players he's given guitars to. I'm kinda surprised he hasn't given you a bass since you're one shy these days." He glanced down at his watch, not waiting for my reply, and said, "Oops, I need to get back. Say, Watson did give you a call, didn't he?"

"Watson?"

"Detective Watson. A born-again hardass from Abilene. His daddy was a Texas Ranger and he's currently the Lieutenant's fair-haired boy."

"I sense a conflict."

"Conflict? Hell, he only thinks liquor, cigarettes, and rock and roll are the tools of Satan. His idea of New Wave was Jim Bakker. No, hell, there's no conflict. Anyway, he was supposed to call you."

"Well, he didn't. What's it about?"

"The cab driver. A witness for you."

"Regarding what?"

"Regarding Sunday night, or should I say, Monday morning. A driver for Harlem Cabs helped Retha Thomas carry you down the hall here to your apartment. He just happened to be dropping off a fare in your building when she drove up. She gave him twenty bucks."

It was like a drink of cold water. I was surprised at the degree of relief I felt. "Damn, that makes a difference. But how'd she know where I lived? I don't remember a damn thing after we left the party."

"Maybe she looked at your driver's license. Maybe she pulled over another drunk and asked him, I don't know."

"Well, whatever. It sure eases my mind."

"I reckon it eases both our minds. As for her having your bass, I guess she forgot she had it, or maybe she was hoping you'd come by for it."

"I can't believe you didn't tell me sooner."

"Sorry, Martin. I've had troubles of my own, and Watson was supposed to call you. Guess he's been too busy." He was bent over, putting his bass back in the case, so I couldn't see his face. Once again, it was hard to tell if he was being sarcastic or sincere. As he snapped the latches shut he looked up. "You're gonna have to get your case fixed, too. Evidently it got jammed in her trunk and she couldn't get it out. The latches broke off, and she just left it in the car, carried the bass up to her room. Maybe somebody saw her carry the bass up to her room like that, tried to take it from her and—"

"Oh, come on . . ."

He shrugged. "Nah, I don't go for that either."

"So do you have any leads?"

"Nothing I can discuss with you. Besides, it's not really my case anymore."

"What do you mean by 'not really'?"

"I guess I'm trying to say the Lieutenant assigned it to Watson." He didn't seem very disturbed about it, but he wouldn't look me in the eye. "Besides," he said, sighing, "it's not really a homicide. Not yet."

"Did you talk to Barbra Quiero?"

"Yeah. Typical LA brat, ain't she? She comes on like she knows everybody and everything, but doesn't know anything that can do us any good."

"She does come on pretty strong."

He shook his head, frowning. "She's too skinny, Martin. I don't trust women like that. They ain't gonna keep you warm on a cold winter night. But it never does get cold in LA, does it?"

Before I could answer, the phone rang. He tried to look disinterested, tugging on the cuffs of the blazer, trying to make it look like it fit. But it never would.

I answered the phone. It was Ladonna. She'd just gotten the flowers. I gave Lasko a good-bye wave.

I showered and shaved. Ladonna was going to take the afternoon off. As I finished dressing I made mental notes. I had a lot of things to do. I wanted to talk to the Thomases to see if they could help me find Retha's boyfriend. I needed to call Leo again. It looked like I was going to have to find a saxophonist. I needed to talk to Vick. But none of these things felt as urgent as seeing Ladonna. I was tying my shoes when the front door swung open. It was Leo.

He looked slightly more rested than the day before, and his hair had been in the vicinity of a comb in the last few hours. He was clean shaven in a white T-shirt, jeans, and sneakers, but when he took off his shades and shook hands with me, I could see that his eyes were still a little puffy.

"How'd it go?" I asked.

He shrugged. "Dinner went OK. Spent sixty-nine dollars at Fonda San Miguel. We talked and stuff."

"Call a cease-fire?"

"I don't know, Martin. I thought maybe we were getting there, but just now when I was driving her to work I got pulled over." He sighed and rolled his eyes. "My license is suspended, you know."

"Outstanding warrants?"

He nodded. "She ended up being two hours late for work 'cause she had to run to the bank so she could bail me out of jail. So she's pissed again. She wants me to give up the Flying V. Fuck that, man, I've always wanted a guitar like that."

I didn't say anything. He dug the American Express card out of his pocket and handed it over. "I don't know if it was worth it or not, but I appreciate the gesture. I'm trying, man, I really am. By the way, something I wanted to tell you. It's about this Retha Thomas deal."

"What?"

He took a labored breath and looked down, not at the floor but not at my face either. "I know you probably have some suspicions about Vick and Ed, but don't hassle them. They didn't have nothing to do with it."

"How would you know?"

"I was with them. Me and Ed left that party not long after you did. I was with them till sunrise."

"So this is something you could testify to in court?"

"No. Why should I? I just told you they didn't have anything to do with it."

"What were you guys doing?"

"None of your business. Just doing some Cuervo shots, mostly."

"That wouldn't sound so bad in court," I said. I watched his face grow more pallid. He put his shades on and headed for the door. "I just wanted to let you know, Martin, so you don't go barking up the wrong tree, pestering people who didn't have nothing to do with anything."

"Nothing at all?" I said.

"Nothing." His hand was on the doorknob, the sunglasses obscuring his eyes.

"Was Donald Rollins with you the other night?"

"Hell, no," he snorted. "I told you—it was just me and them two." He swung the door open.

"You know, Leo, remember when you told me about when you used to shoot at the moon?" He nodded. "You never worried about those bullets falling on somebody else's house, did you?"

He just shrugged and left.

I had a few minutes to kill before Ladonna would get home, so I made some phone calls. I reached Mr. Thomas at the hospital. Retha was no better, no worse. I asked if he or his wife knew the guy that Retha had been seeing. They didn't even know she'd been dating anyone. It was starting to bother me that no one seemed to know much about her. Not her parents, not even her friend, Barbra. When I called the Hyatt, they said Ms. Quiero checked out.

Maybe she'd gone back to LA. I still had a few minutes to kill so I tried reading the paper. There was a short story on page two about Bingo Torres's legal troubles. More record company promotion people and deejays were being questioned about their links to Bingo. Next to the story was a hotel ad offering weekend discounts. It gave me an idea. I called La Quinta and asked for the manager. A man with a soothing baritone came on the line that sounded as if it would please him greatly if he could help me.

I let him know that it would please me, too, in a tone that implied that I expected it, nonetheless. "This is M. Fender down at Lone Star Detectives and Collection Agency? I'm sorting out the last credit charges of a Miss Retha Ann Thomas, who was attacked at your motel last Sunday night. Her father asked for our assistance in clearing up any outstanding bills, things of that nature."

There was a muffled sound as he cleared his throat. "Ah, yes, let me check." He put me on hold and came back on the line a minute later. "Mr. Fender, what sort of irregularities were you looking for? Her bill was paid in full, according to my night manager."

"Well, as you can guess, since there are some questions about what happened, it might be helpful to know how this bill was paid. Credit card, cash . . ."

"Oh, I see. I wonder, could I call you back? We've got a tour bus pulling in the drive just now. I'll gladly call you back at the first opportunity."

I gave him my number. After I hung up, I looked down at the newspaper. One story caught my eye. The headline read: SURGEONS TAKE LARGE TUMOR OUT OF WOMAN. I scanned the text below. A severely overweight woman in California had tried dieting and exercise, resulting in a loss of fifty-five pounds, but she was still grossly overweight, and her midsection refused to taper. After she began bleeding last Friday night, she went to the emergency room and was referred to a gynecologist, who recommended surgery. The next morning, surgeons removed a thirty-pound, watermelon-size tumor from her uterus. It took two surgeons to lift it out. The patient, questioned the day after surgery, was said to be in good spirits, even though tests to determine whether the tumor was malignant had not been completed. She knew before that she was experiencing serious health problems due to her obesity, but now she was relieved to find that something else was wrong. "Who would have known," she said, "that something like that was growing in there?"

I found the story troubling. It was the kind of mundane trivia that seemed to hint at some sort of universal truth. Maybe if I'd had more time on my hands, I could have deciphered its meaning and worked it into a blues song, but it was time to go.

"I'm glad you got a witness," said Ladonna. "I'm sorry the way I acted, I guess I made you feel even worse."

"I'm glad you took the rest of the afternoon off," I said. "That has more than made up for it." She came closer and rested her head on my chest as I reached around on the floor by the bed, looking for my cigarettes. They didn't seem to be there. She kissed my chest. I let my fingers walk under the bed and they bumped into something, but it was soft and silky, definitely not a pack of nonfilter Camels.

"What are you doing?" she asked.

"Looking for my cigarettes. Are they by any chance on that nightstand over there?"

"I thought you quit."

"I did. But I had a relapse."

"Why don't you wait," she said, her hair tickling me as she swept my bare stomach with it, "till after?"

"That'll be the second time I skipped."

"That's what I mean. See what it's like."

It was nice.

———

5

"Did you hear something?" she said.

I opened my eyes. It was dark in the bedroom. We must have dozed off. I got up and peeled the curtain back. No one was outside on the sidewalk, but it sounded like someone was walking down the stairs to the ground level. The shadow made by the two-story complex stretched out across all four rows of the parking lot, meaning the sun had gone almost all the way down.

"I don't see anything," I said, "but I'll bet Michael's getting hungry. I might be, too."

She smiled dreamily and stretched. There was something magical about it. "For what?" she teased.

"How 'bout a li'l Eye-talian?"

"Haven't you had enough?"

"Not nearly," I said.

The kid knew how to make a sandwich, didn't he?

Redfish Veracruzano, fried plantains, and fresh green beans, steamed with butter and garlic just until the snap was gone. Candlelight, birds of paradise, Billie Holiday, single malt Scotch, Ladonna in a negligee. Afterwards, mocha fudge cheesecake, espresso. A cigarette, some more espresso. Ladonna's face, sated but sly under the candlelight. Her abundance of platinum blond tresses, tangled like a passionate argument, held at bay by a white knotted headband.

Dinner was too late for Michael, who'd given up on us and microwaved a pizza. As compensation, he was allowed to watch *Batman* on the VCR in the living room, eating popcorn, drinking diet soda. Whenever one of us stepped in there to ask if he was OK, he rolled his eyes and said, Yeah, sure, of course I'm OK, why wouldn't I be OK?

She didn't want any help with the dishes, so I excused myself and went back in the bedroom to use the telephone. Vick answered right away, still sounding like the hundred grand was tickling his fat stomach. He even called me "pal."

"Just wanted to see if we could square up tomorrow," I said.

"Sure, Martin, sure," he said. "I wanna see you play tomorrow night, anyway."

"Good. I was hoping you weren't going to be lamming out like you said anytime soon."

"No, Martin. I don't know how I could stand to leave this town. You know? I mean, what else do I know?"

"Beats me. I'll see you, then. Maybe right after the gig."

"Fine, pal. I'm going over to the Hyatt now, let Carson from IMF buy me some drinks on his expense account."

I let him go, then called my answering machine. There was a message from Lasko. I called him at home. It wasn't that important, he said, or then again, maybe it was. "Narcotics Division and I are collaborating on something," he said. "A load of big black pills are making the rounds, causing a lot of problems. You remember a couple of cute blond gals used to hang out together at Club Foot a few years ago? Everybody called them the Shimmer Twins?"

"Brenda and Suzanne?"

"Yeah. Both dead. Last night. Found a couple of the big blacks in their makeup bags. Prelims from the lab indicate these pills consist of the same stuff that was in your urine sample, Martin."

"They caused the OD?"

"Yep. Evidently a half of one of these boogers is what most people are taking to party on. Half of one causes people to dive face first in their enchilada dinner, change lanes under a semi, or walk through a glass door. A whole one or at most two is most likely fatal."

"Damn. I guess I was lucky."

"Just thought you'd like to know."

I thanked him as best I could.

I rejoined Ladonna and Michael in the living room. We watched TV together for a couple of hours, then Michael went to bed. I went in with Ladonna as she kissed him good night.

Dark hair, perfect skin, very large eyes looking up at the two of us, he looked like an angel. Ladonna bent over him, holding her negligee together in front so her breasts didn't spill out, an angel's mother. I stood back a couple of steps and turned out the light, feeling just a little out of place.

# 16

When I stepped out the next morning to get the newspaper, there was a note tacked to the door. Big block letters written in that rubbery purplish-red lipstick of hers spelled out the simple message.

**CHICKEN DICK**

Why? Was it jealousy? I didn't think so. Was it because she thought I was laying down on the job, spending time with my girlfriend when I should be out tracking down the guy who tried to murder her friend? I didn't know what to make of it. All I knew for sure was that Barbra Quiero was still in town, still keeping an eye on me, still full of unresolved weirdness. I didn't tell Ladonna about it.

We went to Seis Salsas for brunch. I had *huevos borrachos* and Ladonna had a potato-and-eggs breakfast taco. Michael had *huevos rancheros*.

The South 1st Street restaurant was festive and packed as usual. Mexican bric-a-brac and potted flowers abounded inside, and birds and squirrels romped and hopped from branch to branch on the sprawling oaks outside the window. None of it brought me any cheer.

"Twelve hours ago you were a different guy, Martin," she said. "Don't be a chump."

"Chump?"

"You heard me. You've done your part. You made a two a.m. extortion payoff. You took someone's knockout dose and they almost died anyway. If you just have to do something, maybe you should go tell Lasko about the payoff."

"I just think it's Vick's business, not the police's."

"Vick's business," she said. She shook her head as she dipped a chip in a small cup of chipotle salsa.

"After I drop you guys off," I said, "I'm going to go talk to the IMF Records guy at the Hyatt. The guy who just paid Vick a hundred grand for his little record label."

She looked thoughtfully at Michael, then at me, smiling but disapproving. "You know what I like about you?"

"No. Not all the time."

"You try so hard," she said, "even when you don't know what you're doing."

# 17

A & R stands for "artists and repertoire" and is as common an abbreviation in the music business as CEO is on Wall Street. A strange, often slimy breed, A & R reps are the record company men (rarely women) who walk point; the talent scouts who scour the battle zones, back yards, and hinterlands for tomorrow's platinum-selling artists.

Every week they are expected to sift through hundreds of tapes submitted by anxious bands and dodge phone calls from agents, managers, deejays, record promoters, and disgruntled band members who got the ax just before the deal was signed ("—but we were a *group,* man, this contract only has the singer's name on it").

Some A & R reps turned out to be genuine music fanatics as well as talented wheeler-dealers, people who happened to have a job doing what they loved doing. Others were not so genuine.

Their careers often hang by a slim, gilded thread: sign the next Madonna and you're pronounced a wunderkind, sign two overhyped flops in a row and you drive up one morning to see them stenciling a new name on your designated parking slot.

But none of them seemed to go away for long. Jamie over at EMI would look grim-faced one day because the nu-folk band he signed had stiffed, and Michael at MCA would frantically check his Rolex between each bite of sashimi, waiting for the ax to fall after the new Christian rap artist he signed was arrested for selling crack in Washington Park. Next week, Michael would be ensconced in a new office at Polygram and Jamie would be veep at CBS.

Why did they do it? They had to be streetwise and hip enough to elbow their way past the three-hundred-pound ex-con bouncer at an underground club at four a.m. to see Jane's Addiction, then show up next morning bright-eyed and blow-dried for Messrs. Bottomline, Whatsthedownside, & Faxmethefigures. They had to explain to fashion-victim one-name singers the meaning of "packaging expenses," and they had to explain to stiff-necked CEOs why LA's hottest guitar slinger is in jail for giving a fifteen-year-old girl a "pearl necklace" in the band's dressing room in Bibleville, Alabama.

They had to be obsessive, obstinate, and obstreperous to get the bands and contract concessions they were after. They had to be obtuse and obsequious because it was rarely up to them to say yes, it's hard to say definitely no, and you never say never. They were the hunters and the hunted. People either wanted to buy them a drink or put a bomb in their car. They spent three-quarters of their waking hours on the phone and were experts at avoiding your phone calls.

By living in Austin and playing in a band that already made a living (most of the time) playing music that never went out of style, I had more or less managed to bypass dealing with A & R men. Over the years I'd met between fifty and a hundred of them as they dropped in on our gigs. They knew us by reputation and not rarely would claim to have several of our indie label discs in their record collections. They gave us their cards, occasionally advice, frequently drinks. Some would pump our hands and ask about the pedigree of our instruments, saying, You know, this really isn't my cup of tea, and others would grin widely, slap us on the back and say, Keep it up, man, you guys are the real thing.

It was a compliment I rarely returned.

I had no trouble finding Carson Block. Vick had said he was going to meet him for drinks at the Hyatt the day before. The Hyatt was a favorite stopover for record company people. It turned out that Block was just one of a team of IMF reps who'd come down to deliver the contract and check to Vick, but Block had been the one to initiate the deal and he wanted to personally usher the individual artists into the IMF fold.

He sounded relieved to hear from me when I called. He thought for sure I'd know where he could find Tammy Lynn Johnson, whose R & R Addiction album he was particularly hot on. He wanted to remix a couple of the songs, release them on a three-inch CD for the college market, and send her on tour with a band he'd just signed called Eurotrash. I gave him her number. He was grateful. What could he do for me? I asked him to do me a favor before we met, but I didn't tell him about my after-brunch conversation with the manager of La Quinta Motor Inn. That little bomb I wanted to drop in person.

We met in the Foothills bar of the Hyatt. Oddly enough, the Foothills bar is on the seventeenth floor. The bar on the ground floor, complete with a babbling brook, is called something else. From our corner table, you could see Town Lake and downtown. Tinted a rainy gray by the bar windows, billowy white clouds hovered over the city, puffed up like strutting roosters. Down below, there were sailboats, windsurfers, and rafts on the lake, blankets spread on the grassy shores, joggers and bicyclists chugging around the gravel track. Downtown was well scrubbed and inanimate as a freshly embalmed corpse, with the homeless creeping out of the bushes to sit basking on the benches, watching the grackles, glancing up at the tall empty buildings, staring down at their feet, which were often shod with donated exercise shoes from Goodwill or the Salvation

Army. The Capitol sat twelve blocks away, a sedate granite
statesman taking the weekend off. Just on the other side of the
bridge and across the lake, the Sheraton Crest hugged the north
shore, keeping Vick's Vintage in its shadow.

Carson Block had a plane to catch. He'd sent back his breakfast after catching a whiff of animal fat, he hadn't slept well,
and, worse, he'd left his Filofax back in LA.

"I'm simply lost without it," he explained. The vice president
of A & R for IMF Records wore an unconstructed white summer jacket with a seam down the back and the sleeves rolled
up (neatly) nearly to his elbows, a purple knit shirt with no
emblem over the pocket, and acid-wash jeans. They went with
Nikes like nothing else would.

A diamond stud earring glistened in the lobe of his left ear.
His jeans were creased. Two days' worth of blond stubble made
his face look fuzzy and out of focus, not at all like Don Johnson.
His hair was parted on the side and just barely touched his
shoulders when he tilted his head. When he moved, the jacket
folded up or angled oddly, making it look like his torso was in
danger of collapsing. This man was a tastemaker, I reminded
myself. I felt sorry for the bands he'd just signed.

"So you did what I asked?" I said.

He nodded, chewing one side of his lower lip. This gesture,
I found out later, would pass for an emotive response.

"And she didn't work for you, ever?"

"No," he said coolly. "And as far as my assistant can determine, she hasn't applied for a job with the company in the last
six months. We usually try to keep applications for that long,
but you can imagine how many applicants we get, so . . ." He
let it hang, turning his palms up, helpless.

He'd already let me know what a wonderful favor it was he'd
done me, considering the fact that it was the weekend. Luckily,
his administrative assistant was down at his office pulling phone
numbers out of his Filofax for him when I'd called him.

"I just find it strange," I said, "that a girl comes here from

LA—a girl who was trying to get a job at a record company—asks a lot of questions about a guy that you want to give a hundred thousand dollars to for a record label, and then someone tries to kill her, and you . . ."

His face turned red. It clashed with his purple shirt. "I *don't* know *what* you're implying . . ."

"Cool it," I said. "I'm not sure either. But like someone said, I try especially hard when I don't know what I'm doing."

I pushed my chair back and took in the view again. It was too peaceful outside, too subdued inside. Carson Block was waving to the waitress with IMF Records' platinum American Express card. It was time to stir things up.

"Hey, Carson, why don't you use the Visa card you used for Retha Thomas's room at La Quinta? Or is it maxed out?"

The waitress had arrived and was reaching for the American Express card. Carson snatched it back and said, "Would you like something? A beer maybe?"

The motel manager had been quite helpful. I chalked up part of my success in the matter to my experience at the collection agency. People often think they can get away with anything. They get a great idea, they make plans, they forget about the paper trail. Retha Thomas's motel room was paid for by Carson Block's Visa card, as was her rental car. One day last week, she'd had a visitor. This visitor had ordered drinks and paid for them with a MasterCard. The MasterCard was in the name of one B. Q. Torres. Either that night or soon after, she'd had a visitor whose description fit Barbra Quiero to a T. I was anxious to talk to the incommunicado Detective Watson about these facts. But first—

"I don't know this other girl you're talking about," he said, sipping his beer, swallowing with difficulty. "And I don't know how this could be related to what happened to Retha Thomas."

"Retha wanted a job. You liked her but you didn't have a position for her. You led her on. You asked her how she'd like an expenses-paid trip to a rocking little burg on the Colorado River. All she had to do was find out just how deeply Vick Travis was connected to Bingo Torres. Am I right so far?"

"Look, Martin, I brought this deal to the company, so my butt was in a sling. The deal had gone too far to pull out when I heard about Vick being possibly tainted with this payola thing. I don't have to tell you . . ."

"You'd lose your job," I said. "But you didn't want to lose the deal either. That's why you showed a little initiative."

He nodded, chewing one side of his lower lip.

"What did she find out?" I asked.

He palmed the beer glass with his hands, speaking quietly. "She had the whole picture Wednesday of last week when she called me. It didn't sound like much of a downside. Bingo paid for a few recording sessions for Vick's artists, using the name he used to perform under, Danny Cortez. So what? We're talking small change stuff here, Martin, and the way I understand it, other than these deals, Vick hasn't been closely tied with Bingo for a long time, not since the '60s."

"When was the last time you saw Retha Thomas?"

"In a bar in Hollywood, about three weeks ago. I asked her if she was interested in playing detective for me, and she was. You know the rest."

"Do I?"

He chewed his lip, somewhat forcefully this time, and his eyes widened. I nearly laughed. "If you think I'd try to kill somebody just to cover my tracks on a puny little record deal . . ."

"So puny that you hire an amateur private detective? So puny that you fly here in person to deliver a check for a hundred thousand dollars?"

He rolled his eyes and waved for the check again. I settled back in my seat and thought about how much I disliked him. He cleared his throat and adjusted his shoulders under the flimsy jacket.

"Look, I know it seems awfully sleazy. This job . . . It isn't always easy, and it isn't all fun and nice to look at from the inside, either. But believe me, I'm a fan. That's why I do it. I'm not in this to hang around with a bunch of suits—accountants, lawyers, con artists, even amateur detectives sometimes. Sometimes you have to wade through a lot of sleazy bullshit or nobody would ever hear the music. And that'd be a shame."

"Speaking of lawyers," I said, "might the friendly legal staff at IMF Records come to Bingo's rescue, if it would be to everybody's benefit?"

"Maybe. Maybe not."

I was glad he didn't say yes, and didn't say no. It would have been out of character.

I got a handful of quarters at the front desk and took them to the pay phone to try out an idea I had. I checked my watch. It was eleven. That made it nine on the West Coast. I got Retha Thomas's credit record printout from my jacket and called her bank in LA. I told the girl in the accounts department that I was calling from Lone Star Detectives and Collection Agency and that it was kind of important.

I gave her Retha Thomas's account number and she looked it up. Was there any unusual activity? I asked. She hummed while she looked it over. Her humming did nothing to soothe the questions that buzzed in my brain. Retha was done with her fact-finding mission Wednesday of last week, half a week before I got back to town. Why did she stick around? Was someone else paying her, too?

"No, not really," said the clerk. "In fact, the only activity over the last three weeks are these two deposits, both last week. One Friday, for eight hundred dollars, and then Wednesday, for five hundred."

"How were they made?" I asked.

"They were deposited in an automatic teller machine in Austin," she said. "How's the weather down there? Hot, I'll bet."

"You can fry an egg on the sidewalk," I said. It was a lie. It never gets that hot anywhere where they have sidewalks. And besides, I was feeling a distinct chill.

"How'd you find me?" she asked. She was just out of the shower, in a white terry-cloth bathrobe. Tendrils of damp, just-toweled-off hair stuck up more than ever on top, and a few curved in toward her face like long thorns. We were on the fourth floor of the Radisson, a downtown glass pyramid that was a sort of skeletal ice palace version of the Hyatt's traditional atrium design.

"It just took a few quarters, Barbra," I said.

"Glad to see you finally made it out of bed." She sat down by the window, cracked the curtain, peeked out, then let it fall shut.

"I got your message."

"Did you? You don't care. I can see you don't really give a damn about finding out what happened to Retha. You spend all day in bed with that bimbo and the rest of the time you probably hang around with that tubby pervert and his Igor."

I took a step back. "That girl is not a bimbo, and I'm getting a little bit weary of this confrontational relationship of ours. I still get the distinct impression that you'd like to hold me responsible for what happened to Retha."

She gulped hard and looked away. Being wet and without makeup took away some of her hard edges. She had a sort of raw, benignly foreign look to her, as opposed to the hard, exotic impression she gave off fully coiffed and polished. In fact, she reminded me a little of some of the lighter-skinned Mayan women I'd seen the last time I'd been in Mexico. I felt an urge to ask where her family was from, and I wondered what she looked like when she was a little girl, where she went to school. But I swallowed those curiosities, chalking them up to the weird chemistry of our personalities, the close quarters, and her being in a damp bathrobe.

"Look," I said. "Retha was here on behalf of IMF Records to check out Vick Travis's ties to Bingo Torres, a South Texas record promoter who's hip deep in a payola scandal that would have queered the record deal that went down with IMF yesterday. I found out that Retha wired thirteen hundred dollars cash to her bank account back home. That means something, although I'm not sure what."

Her eyes flashed as she looked up at me, irritated. "She doesn't know a soul in town yet she's able to wire thirteen hundred dollars cash home and you say you don't know what it means? It means someone here was giving her money, chicken dick. That fat son of a bitch that you've been working for is probably the guy. She probably decided to use what she had on him, he got tired of paying her off and had her killed. Maybe you were in on it."

"Maybe *you* were in on it," I snapped. "Is that why you were here last week?"

She drew the folds of the robe in closer and shook her head. "Oh God, no, Martin. She was my *friend,* for chrissake. She called me last week and she sounded funny. I knew she was up to something and she didn't know what she was doing. I got in on Thursday, but I didn't catch up with her until it was too late, and that's the truth. I went by her room at La Quinta, but she wasn't in, and that's as close as I got until the hospital."

"All right. Maybe she cut a little deal of her own with Vick to keep quiet about the payola thing. That'd be a shame, because a couple of guys got a lot more for it than she did."

"And you don't know who the couple of guys are, do you?"

I shook my head.

"And the police don't know anything about this angle, do they?"

"No, not yet." I suddenly felt stupid, inadequate. Between the drawn curtains and the wet girl, the room felt claustrophobic. I wanted to get out of there, but not until I had resolved to do something *right* for a change. As weary as I was of Barbra's chronic suspicion and mercurial outbursts, I didn't want to expose her to the same kind of risk her friend had stumbled into. She was bound to be precious to someone.

"I read the papers, Martin. I get the picture. I know that Bingo Torres is one dangerous Mexican. Just because Vick got his deal without any exposure doesn't mean Bingo would appreciate people sticking their noses where they don't belong. You'd better stay away from him."

"I plan on it."

"Well, what else can we do?"

"You should dry your hair, and I need to get ready for a gig tonight. I'll check on you afterwards. If you want, we can go to the police in the morning. How's that?"

"Going to the police is fine with me, Martin. I want to know why what happened to Retha happened, and I want the people who did it to pay. You haven't done your part yet."

"There you go again . . ." I said, but didn't finish.

She was shaking. She looked around the room, at the four walls, at my feet, a lot of white showing in her eyes. "I wish you weren't playing tonight. I'm scared to go out. Men are still following me."

"Just wait here for me, OK?"

She nodded. "Don't forget about me. Or Retha."

That was not likely.


I didn't know who would be following Barbra Quiero. I didn't want it to be Bingo's men, but I couldn't imagine who else it would be. Something wasn't quite right. Bingo had warned me that he'd deal harshly with anyone who was thinking about testifying against him. Maybe Retha hadn't taken his warning seriously enough.

But why would Bingo's men be following Barbra? The deal with IMF was done, history. She'd have nothing to gain by exposing Vick's relationship with Bingo. And Bingo had little to fear from the exposure of his ties to Vick. Or did he? Maybe something besides payola was the dirty laundry here.

There was also something off-key about Barbra's suggestion that *Vick* tried to have Retha killed over the exposure of his ties to Bingo. He'd told me about their association, and I hadn't felt like my life was in danger. Besides, Leo had alibied Vick and Ed.

But that gave me little comfort. When I got home I gave Leo a call. Nadine said he'd gone to sound check. Sound check? We never did a sound check at Antone's. We'd played there five hundred times, for chrissakes. They just got a new PA system, she said, everyone's been trying to call you—don't you check your answering machine anymore? I fed the cat, packed up the Danelectro, and headed over there.

As I crossed the lake a plane flew overhead, heading west. I wondered if Carson Block was on it. I also wondered if the rest of the IMF crew had gone back to LA. Maybe they were keeping an eye on Barbra. I checked my rearview mirror. As I changed lanes, a late model Ford changed lanes, too. I wondered if someone was keeping an eye on me.

# 19

"MIKE CHECK, CHECK ONE TWO."

Bam, BAM, buh-duh-duh, buh-duh-duh, BAM-BAM, BOOM.

"MIKE CHECK, CHECK ONE TWO, CHECK."

Some people may assume that a band just shows up at the club a few minutes before show time, has a couple of cocktails and cigarettes, and saunters onstage, plugs in, and lets the magic happen. Sometimes we did it that way, more or less. Especially in Austin at a familiar venue or on the road at a club with a good sound system and staff. On those occasions, the roadies would go down to the club and set up the gear while the band showered, shaved, dressed, and let the road kinks fall out. Then there were the occasions where we didn't know what kind of sound system, acoustics, or people we'd be dealing with. Sometimes the club manager or promoter would need a bit of schmoozing, or maybe even a show of force. Then the sound check could present all sorts of opportunities, between watching the roadies rewire the club's equipment, playing pool or video games, doing an interview, or just meeting some of the locals. Sometimes we jammed and had even been known to write a decent song or two during an impromptu rehearsal in front of a happy hour crowd.

Then there were the times when the PA didn't work. Or the club manager tried to renegotiate our contract after we pulled in. Or an amp didn't work, or one of us was hung over or just plain pissed off and we'd have an argument in front of people we didn't know.

Buh-DOOM, buh-DOOM, DOOM, DOOM, DOOM.

Doom-CRACK, doo-doom-doom-CRACK, doom-CRACK, doo-doom-doom-CRACK, bip, bip, bip, buh-DOOM-DOOM-CRACK.

This was not one of those sound checks where we sat and reminisced, jammed, or played pool. Ray was late but Leo was actually drinking a soft drink and behaving himself, and the roadies were working hard. The equalization curve wasn't set right on the sound system, and Nick was having a hard time figuring out how to adjust it on the new mixing console. The drums sounded good and loud, but there was a gut-wrenching low-frequency ring that would set the woofers roaring with feedback. It was a sound that tickled the soles of my feet, rattled the strings of my bass as it lay across my lap, and made my stomach want to roll over.

This sound check was hell, and the feedback wasn't the only thing making my stomach turn. Detective Tom Watson was sitting next to me at a table in the back of the club. He'd followed me there in his late model Ford, an unmarked police car—the car I'd seen in my rearview mirror.

Watson had short iron-gray hair and a neatly trimmed regulation straight-line mustache of the same color that accentuated the drooping form of a thin-lipped mouth. His blue eyes gleamed with alertness, and the nostrils on his slightly aquiline nose flared frequently when he talked. His shoulders were broad, his posture perfect. I remembered Lasko's thumbnail sketch: Abilene native, son of a Texas Ranger, born-again hardass. It fit.

He waved another gory 8 × 10 in front of my face. "See these spatter marks down in the corner?" I nodded. "Now look at this," he said, handing me an X ray of Retha Thomas's skull.

"See the crushing wound? See the angle? That straight line was caused by the impact of the body of your bass guitar hitting her near straight on. Back of her skull."

"What does it mean?" I said.

"This was the first blow, son. She had her back turned, standing, when it happened. Maybe she knew the person. After she was hit once, she started to fall and was hit again, in the front of her face, and her chest. The pattern and shape of the droplets on the wall shows that, shows what angle the weapon came down, and so forth."

He pulled out another 8 × 10. Seen in a black-and-white closeup, the sawtooth-edged droplets looked like black suns. Another photo showed the corner by the door. There the spatters were in the shape of tadpoles, their skinny tails pointing out the direction they had come from. "She curled up in a fetal position here," he said, "but the perp kept hitting her. The rest of the wounds bear the peculiar outline of the neck of the instrument, with little notch marks made by the frets."

The next photo was of the bed. The sheets were blotched with blood. Her clothes were wadded up against the headboard. Retha wasn't in it. These photos were taken after she'd been taken to the hospital.

"We know that she was in bed after the attack, not before," he said. "And she was in no condition to get there on her own. The perpetrator put her there and ripped off her clothes to make it look like a sex-related crime. It doesn't mean it wasn't, but there was no vaginal penetration, no semen in any of her body cavities."

"I hope she lives," I said. It was a redundant remark, but I felt obligated to inject some hope into the conversation.

"So do I," he said. "On the other hand, I know it may sound cold, but we'd know a lot more if she'd been killed, the way it turns out. We can lift fingerprints from a corpse, you know, using superglue fumes, a hair dryer, and orange dye. We can cut open your stomach and determine whether you had lunch at the Night Hawk or Threadgill's. But the doctors and paramedics were concerned with saving her life instead of preserving evidence. That's how it ought to be, but the crime scene was pretty well trampled, and we have to make do with X rays and doctor's reports and what you see here in these photos. Plus a little luck and a lot of shoe leather."

He wrinkled his nose as he looked around the bar. I got the impression that he never set foot inside one unless it was pertinent to his job. "You know anything about murder?" he asked.

"I've seen victims up close, and I've seen people get shot. Is that what you mean?"

He shook his head, shuffling the photos and putting them back in their folder. "Nah, I'm talking about killing, why and how and when. This is a blunt instrument case. This kind of killing goes all the way back to the day Cain slew Abel. A poker game goes sour and the next thing you know the loser has a table leg in his hand dripping blood and brains. An English professor blows up at his wife for breaking his favorite meerschaum pipe and he picks up the fireplace poker and parts her hair with it. A gun is a whole 'nother matter. You carry a gun, you've already got some of the mindset in place to kill, and when you do it, there's some distance between you and the victim. You can even pretend that it was the gun that did it, that drove you crazy.

"But a blunt instrument is different. You might pick it up and start bashing before you realize what you done. So you gotta be mad, you gotta be in a murderous rage. It's liable to be messy as hell, and if you're determined to do the job, it generally takes more than one whack."

As if to punctuate the remark, a rapid-fire roll of the drums cannoned through the speakers, rattling the ashtray on the table as well as my nerves. Watson scowled at the stage, then at me.

"Lemme see that bass," he said.

I handed him the Danelectro. "This is a different brand," I said.

"I know," he snarled. "The other one was a Fender. Just

like your name." He paused for effect, then turned his attention to the instrument, gripping the neck with both hands, hefting it upside down like a club. "Doesn't matter. See, this is how the weapon was held for the first couple of blows. Then the perpetrator lost his grip and dropped it or it flew out of his hands."

He put the bass down on the table, then picked it up by gripping the curved sides of the body, moving it in a short arc. "See," he said, "the way the neck marks got on her body must have been when the perp held the weapon like *this*."

It looked awkward and it felt awkward, watching him hold the Danelectro like that, and trying to think about trying to hit someone like that, but still the images came. And they were not pleasant.

He put the bass down and looked at me, poker-faced.

"What does this mean?" I said.

"I don't know. I just know it happened that way. I don't know why and I don't know who, but I know that's the way it happened. The perp—who was your height, give or take a half a foot—lost his grip and picked it up again by the body. In the meantime, the victim crawled or stumbled across the room. It was lucky, actually, because the firmer grip and better swing he had going with the first couple of blows were offset slightly by the fact the victim was standing, and her head was able to move with the blow. When she was crumpled up on the floor against the wall is when she could've really got her brains splattered. Here," he said, picking up the bass by the neck. I took it and put the strap back on the pegs and slung it over my shoulder.

He looked pleased with the image, as if I'd just put my own noose around my neck.

"He kept hitting her after she was balled up in the corner," he said. "Another reason for hitting her with this other grip was probably because of the awkward angle there in the corner. And that indicates to me that he knew what he was doing, he wasn't just mad, he wanted to make sure he got the job done."

He looked at me like he was daring me to disagree with his conclusions. I said nothing.

"I don't like you, Fender," he said. "I don't like you at all, and I'm under no obligation to treat you kindly. I get the same paycheck whether the crime was committed against a decent person or scum, and more often than not, things like this are perpetrated against people like you. And that's no coincidence. This is my job and I don't have to bullshit you."

"Is that what you came here to tell me, or were you just trying to gross me out with these photos?"

He sucked in his lower lip, making a clucking sound. "You think you're some kind of wiseass and you pal around with Lasko thinking that gives you some sorta carte blanche, but it doesn't. You're an ordinary citizen, not a cop, and what's more, you're a sinful heathen. I came here to tell you I don't want you calling motel managers under false pretenses trying to do my job for me. And I don't want you hanging around with Bingo Torres. He's got enough trouble."

"So you know Retha had a visitor by the name of B. Q. Torres, and she was here on behalf of IMF—"

"Yeah, yeah, yeah, I know all that. But I don't think Bingo left his house Sunday night. He's just about to be indicted by the grand jury and has been under what you might call a watchful eye, you know."

"Meaning he's under surveillance and you know for a fact that he didn't leave home?"

He shook his head slightly, winking his left eye. "I said he *was* under surveillance. The feds have been dragging their feet, and we've had a manpower shortage ourselves, so surveillance has been spotty at times. Besides, he's awfully cagey."

"You didn't answer my question about whether he left the house Sunday night. Did he?"

"No, I didn't. I didn't even say if I knew if he did or not. I just said I didn't *think* he left."

"And if you knew, you wouldn't necessarily tell me about

it." He nodded. As far as nonanswers go, he had Carson Block beat. "What about the record company guys?"

"I'm checking them out." He slid his chair back and got up, hitched up his pants, and buttoned his jacket. Not, however, before giving me a generous glimpse of his shoulder holster and handcuffs. "Lemme tell you something, Fender, and I hope it's the last time I have to tell you. I got a job to do, and I don't need your help. You got your own job, scummy as it is."

"MIKE CHECK, MIKE CHECK, TESTING ONE-TWO," came Nick's voice, thundering over the PA. "Martin, are you ready? MARTIN FENDER TO THE BANDSTAND, PLEASE."

"Looks like they want you," said Watson.

"Yeah," I said. I got up and held the neck of the bass up straight so it wouldn't hit anything as I walked up to the stage.

The next time I looked back he was still standing there, glaring at me. A waitress approached him with a drink tray, but he brushed her off with a cold stare.

# 20

The low notes rumbled out of my bass like the growls of an angry dog. "Route 66," "Spoonful," "Shakin' All Over," "Hellhounds on My Trail." The strap cut into my shoulder like that angry dog's leash. "Mannish Boy," "What a Woman," "Take Me to the River." By midnight Antone's was packed with crinoline skirts and leather jackets and halter tops and pinstripe suits and 501 button flies and wing tips and beaded cocktail dresses. Conk-crowned heads mingled with high flies, Stetsons, stingy brims, gimme caps, and beehives. In other words, the usual eclectic mix in the usual swirls of smoke.

Clifford Antone, godfather of the Austin blues scene, came out of his office, white shirt collar spread open wide over the lapels of his black suit, nodding approval. The long-legged queen of R & B, Lou Ann Barton, stood at his side, nursing a tall cocktail and crushing a cigarette under one stiletto heel.

Ladonna and Michael were there, Lasko and Barbra Quiero were not. A beaming, rotund Vick Travis trundled up in his leather jacket, and a caveman Ed the Head in a white bib shirt and black tux jacket sat next to the mixing board, midway between the dance floor and the front of the club. The halogen lamp over the console sprayed out over Vick's table, so I was able to keep an eye on him. Like a guard dog.

Billy kept the beat steady and sweaty, a mileage logbook sticking out of his back pocket. Ray blew his horn like a pomade-slick demon from hell, turning a cold shoulder on the other band members, especially Leo. Leo ignored Ray too, and played well despite the cast on his hand. Sometime between sound check and the first song, he'd switched from sodas to Jack Daniel's. Nadine wobbled on a stool by the dressing room door. She spent more time looking down at the blue drink in her hand than she did looking up at us. The wound was still there, whatever it was. My bass kept growling.

Oh, man. Saturday night and it had been a hell of a week. I felt like I was in a different dimension, standing up there onstage after all that had happened. I felt like a man inside a television. I told myself it was just a combination of mood and too-bright lights in my eyes as I watched the people who were watching us. I told myself it was just an illusion. But it wasn't.

"Who Put the Sting on the Honey Bee," "Born Lover," "The Crawl," "Cadillac Daddy."

The bass notes shook the room like thunder: Vick would look at Leo and his new guitar, and Leo would look up from it and Vick would look away. Ed the Head looked hard and compact and menacing, a baboon in a tuxedo. People would pass by Vick's table and he would give a robust laugh, pumping their hands, insisting that he buy them a drink, then erupt again, as if that was the funniest thing in the world. Then he'd look back up at the stage, and I knew. He was watching me. Not just what I played, or my face, or my clothes. But something, some part of me. More than once I checked to see if my fly was down. It was not a healthy feeling.

Bingo Torres came in during the last song before our break. The two cronies I'd seen poolside, Roberto and Nameless, followed in his shadow. Bingo seemed to be looking up toward stage right, Leo's side. When Leo stepped up to the mike to sing "Trailer Park Babe," Bingo appeared to shake his head with disgust, elbowing Roberto, pointing. Soon the thrift shop proprietor maneuvered his heavy torso around to see who was standing behind him, and the Payola King appeared to look at him like the sole of a shoe looks at the back of a cockroach.

That was when I knew that there was something to the weird sensation of being a man inside a television set. Some of these characters were watching us, wearing their secrets on their faces, unaware or just not caring that I noticed. I felt like an actor onstage, suddenly realizing that some of the actors in the play were reading from scripts that were different than mine. But as I studied the psychic interplay between Bingo, Vick, and Leo, I had the feeling that I was about to be able to read between the lines.

We went one more time on the chorus, held up on the root while Leo scratched out a descending pattern starting on the fifth, clanged out the root chord, and waited for a buh-duh-dum on Billy's rack and snare and we were done. As the MC announced that we'd be right back after a short break, the stage floor began to shake with deep, rolling feedback. Nick trotted up to the stage to see what was wrong.

I leaned my bass in its stand and turned off the power switch on my amp. I didn't want it to overheat.

I hung my jacket on a hook in the dressing room, toweled off with a sour-smelling bar rag, and let Leo bum a cigarette. Ray and Billy ducked out ahead of us, and the tiny dressing room was soon as empty as it was ugly. The set had gone well, but there was either too much or too little that the four of us could say to one another at that point in time.

I walked Ladonna to her car.

"You sound good tonight," she said. Michael skipped on ahead of us.

"Thanks," I said. "And you look damn good. I don't usually line anything up during breaks, but maybe I should get your number, sweet thing."

She laughed, tugging my arm, walking briskly through the parking lot. She was tired and Michael needed to get to bed, but she wasn't anxious to leave. Maybe she hadn't been able to see the way that Vick was looking at Leo, or the way that

Bingo was looking at the two of them, but she knew I'd seen things in a way that I hadn't seen them before.

"And there's something else," she said as she unlocked her door and got in. "You're hard, Martin, like you've taken a drug. But I know you don't take drugs, so I know what it is."

I didn't deny I had a gun.

"A gun is a bad idea waiting to happen, Martin," she said. "Statistically, just carrying a gun increases your chances of getting shot."

"A gun is a gun, and it's just there, in my guitar case. I'm here, I'm me, and I'm not a gun-toting maniac."

She gave me one of her long meaningful looks, then put the keys in the ignition and made sure that Michael had fastened his seat belt. After accepting a kiss, she locked the doors and said, "You're going to see Vick after?"

"Yeah," I said, "I've got to. Don't worry."

"OK." But she didn't mean it. We kissed again, and she put her meaning there.

We rushed through the last set. It wasn't sloppy or soulless, but it lacked. It lacked a bit of funk as the rhythms stumbled over the groove, and the tempos rushed along feverishly, like we were running from something.

But midway during the instrumental section of "Nails in My Heart," Leo's tone began to soar. He overcame the sluggishness of his right-hand attack by squeezing more vibrato-strangled sound out of his fretting fingers. The notes seemed to be crying out a painful confession. High up on the neck the fingers climbed, feedback threatening, sweat pouring off his face. He climaxed with a long, four-note wail wrenched out of the same fret position, then raked his pick down the neck to the nut, whanged an open chord, and fell back against his amp. Ray growled out the melody on his sax for the last twelve bars, and we ended the song. After a round of applause and a muttered thank you, we launched into the last song and a perfunctory encore. But they were ordinary and as earthbound as most of the rest of the set had been, and once again, I felt like we had cheated our audience.

We got paid anyway, of course, and I divided the cash into equal amounts after deducting Nick and Steve's cuts, minus their advances. Billy marked down the amount in his ledger, Ray folded his share in a gold money clip and started to walk out to his Buick, where Kate would be sitting impatiently, her nose in the air, punching the buttons on the radio with black lacquered nails. I hadn't paid Leo yet. I asked Ray to wait up.

He stopped in the tracks of his creepers just long enough to spit over the padded shoulder of his jacket: "What?"

"Is that it, Ray?" I asked. "If you're walking, I'd like to know why."

"Ask Leo." With that, he started walking again, and didn't look back.

Leo, pale-faced and sweaty, was coming out of the dressing room. Nadine was still in there. He saw the look on my face and started to turn back. I hurried over and grabbed his sleeve. "What is it, Leo?"

"What is what?"

"Why does everybody say, Ask Leo?"

The dark circles didn't soften the panic in his eyes, and the surliness in his voice didn't pass for bravery. "Maybe they think I know everything."

"How'd you get that Flying V?"

"Whaddya mean?"

"You got a new guitar, and I know you didn't come off the road with enough money to buy one. You also got a broken hand and a very upset girlfriend, all in one day. And I saw the way that Vick was looking at you. Is Vick your banker, your boyfriend, or what?"

"Fuck you, Martin," he blurted, and pulled away so that his sleeve ripped off in my hand. He looked at the damage, then me. "You guys, man. Ray's a goddamn West Texas puritan and you're a goddamn hardass. Just a rock solid dude. Aren't ya? Even after some chick gets bashed up with your guitar.

You don't know shit, you don't understand a goddamn thing."
He leaned into my face. "Not. a goddamn thing."

Then he backed away toward the dressing room door. He
looked like he wanted to say something else as a big fat tear
ran out from the corner of his eye and shot down by his nose.
He spun and hit the exit door and bolted through it. I held it
open and looked out and saw him sprint across Guadalupe,
dodging cars, then disappear around a corner.

The club was empty except for a couple of guys with mops,
the sound man, and Clifford Antone, hands in his pockets,
asking Nadine if she wanted him to call a cab. I gave her Leo's
money. I felt bad for her. She grabbed my hand.

"Did you see his cast?" she said, sobbing.

"What about it?"

"Bingo made him let him sign it. He wrote, 'Another gift
from Vick Travis.' A heart around it and everything."

She put her head down in her hands and cried. Clifford put
his arm around her and nodded at me. He'd take care of her.

I got out of there as quickly as I could. I felt soiled by shame—
Leo's shame, for sinking so low that he would get his hand
broken over a debt, and my shame, for not catching his fall.

When I got to the car with my bass, Barbra Quiero was in
the passenger seat.

"I had to know," she was saying, "I just had to know."

The traffic was light but awkward, the drivers overly careful
as they left the clubs smelling like DWIs. Some of the traffic
lights had switched over to blinking amber or red after midnight, making the city seem like it was sleeping with one eye
open. I was wary, too, gripping the steering wheel with a white-
knuckled grip to keep my hands from shaking.

My damp clothes clung. In the morning they'd smell like a
million cigarettes. The three a.m. air felt leaden, even with the
top down, peeled back on a murky sky. Barbra's words seemed
to fall into a deadened void quickly after she spoke them, as if
the night were too tired for resonance.

Six days before I'd taken a ride with her friend after my first gig back in my hometown. Hometown. I'd felt like a stranger here. Now it was feeling a bit more familiar again as we took Martin Luther King, Jr., Boulevard, then Red River back into downtown. But instead of a cozy feeling, it felt like a bad déjà vu.

"That flashy Mexican guy," she was saying, "was Bingo Torres?" I nodded yes, that was his name. "One of the guys who was with him is one of the guys that have been following me the past few days, off and on."

We pulled up in front of the Radisson lobby. "Well, now we know," I said. "You'd better stay in your room."

"I will," she said. She grabbed me and pulled me to her. She was shaking, her body cold and clammy. She wouldn't let go. Finally I pried her away. "Maybe I should go up with you," I said. She nodded. I put the hazard lights on, got out and opened her door for her, and escorted her through the lobby, to the elevator, and down the hall to her room. I unlocked the door for her and checked out the room. It was empty.

"OK?" I said.

"OK." I started to give her room key back but she wouldn't take it. "Maybe you'll want to come back before tomorrow morning."

"Now look . . ."

"Martin," she began, then hesitated. She grabbed my arm and pulled me to her. "I've got a feeling. I don't know, it's a bad feeling."

"Relax. I think I know what this is all about now. I'm going to Vick's. I'll be back in the morning."

She relaxed her grip, but not before grinding her crotch into me and biting my ear. When I pulled away, she had that don't-forget-about-me look. I left her room in a hurry.

A bell captain was giving the Ghia a dirty look when I got downstairs. I turned it around and headed over to Vick's.

I stuffed my gun in the back of my pants before I went in.

# 21

"Just don't try to analyze everything," said Vick, sitting at the card table. "Take it easy. Have a drink. We're your friends. You go around asking questions all the time, you're never gonna hear the answers. Come on, have a cigarette. I just sold my record company, man. This is the end of an era." A fat pearl of sweat crawled down the side of his face. His damp curly hair was freshly clawed back on his head, but one strand had already broken loose, hanging over his left eye like a dead tree limb. He blew at it from the corner of his mouth as he poured another shot of Cuervo, sloshing it, laughing silently, waving the bottle at me.

"End of an era, Martin. End of a goddamn era."

I poured a slug and knocked it back. Vick slid his cigarette pack at me. I shoved them back and lit one of my own. He closed his hand over his pack, shook one out, put it between his lips, and set fire to it. He closed his eyes as he filled up with smoke, gradually letting it curl out from his nostrils and stream out between his teeth.

Ed the Head stood off to the side, his shirt still buttoned up to the top, a knotty Adam's apple moving up and down above it. He was monkeying around with the tape deck, adjusting the bass level until the low woofs rattled the room. He bobbed his head to the beat, eyelids drooping down, head lolling back, body convulsing slowly in a dance that was part "Hullaballoo," part epilepsy. Just as it looked like he was going to teeter over backward, he'd open his eyes wide and give us a goofy grin and wheezy giggle. He was just playing.

I sat on the other side of the table, slowly sipping another shot of Cuervo in the hopes that it would make my heart stop charging up against my rib cage. I looked over to the poster of Keith Richard nodding out, oblivious to everything except the movie playing on the inside of his eyelids. What was that like, I wondered, to be totally anesthetized? To have everything blotted out, every pain, every responsibility. Was that like being dead? Was that what everyone craved? Escape—temporary but total—in convenient doses?

A few shots of Cuervo did no more than coat the rough edges. Everybody needed a little something to help them get through, but the serious escape artists had to have something to get them all the way through to the other side.

Vick sat smiling like a truckstop Buddha, tequila glistening on his lips, eyeing me like I was a long-lost friend, petting his stomach like it was a child napping on his lap. Maybe I had died and gone to hell.

The music from Antone's still throbbed in my head and rang in my ears. My plucking fingers tingled, and my shoulder burned where the strap had cut in. I had a vague sensation that I was floating. Maybe music was a form of death too. People wire themselves up to your beat, plugging into a common consciousness. The melody soothes the pain, the rhythm massages the soul. They escape, maybe for three minutes, maybe for a few hours, then they're back in the cold world again, not dancing. And I was here, in this ugly place, knowing that things were about to come to an ugly head.

The thoughts of death and anesthesia were a side issue. I knew I was in that insular, sweaty little room to get at the truth, the ugly hard kernel of facts at the center of all the trouble I'd stumbled into since our van had rolled back into town. But getting at the truth was tough because everyone was running from it, shrugging it off, or trying to buy protection from it. Donald Rollins had ducked out from under it with a dose of heroin. Leo was running from it, trying to drink it into submission. Ray snubbed it and wouldn't have anything to do with it. Bingo Torres tried to bully it with his smarmy machismo. Retha had confronted it somehow, only to have it come crashing down on her. Vick had bought a little time away from it, then came out seeming practically unscathed. And that just didn't seem right.

I looked at Keith Richard and felt irritated at him for being asleep on the job, nodding out through the disintegration of rock and roll. I thought about the fat lady with the thirty-pound tumor, relieved to find that the problem was *something else,* something that was now apart from her and had never been her fault to begin with. I looked at Vick and Ed and shook my head with disgust.

The tape segued into an Albert Collins song, and Vick grinned with satisfaction on hearing it. "Oh, yeah," he said, "that there is some good music." He looked at me for acknowledgment. "Huh? Am I right?"

He knew I wasn't going to argue with that. I just sat there, sipping the tequila, smoking, feeling ready to explode.

Vick tilted his head back as if the guitar player were playing overhead, suspended from the ceiling. "Oh, man, that man can play that guitar. You know? No wonder they call him the Ice-picker. It's almost like there's no tone on that ax, no treble, no bass, just the naked sound of those top strings thwacking against the neck." He brought his gaze back down to eye level, smiling at me. "Almost sounds like he's spanking that guitar, pinching it to make it go *ouch.* You know what I mean, Martin?"

"Don't ruin it for me," I said. "I'm a fan of Albert Collins, and I don't want to have to think of your perverted fantasies every time I hear one of his songs."

"Aw, come on, Martin. Who you calling a pervert, huh?"

"You, you fat bastard."

He sighed, rubbing his stomach. He looked at the Cuervo bottle, thought it over for a second, and poured another shot. He set the bottle down, pinched the shot glass between his thumb and forefinger, and sent it home. The liquor elicited a small tremor within his huge bulk, which he acknowledged with a short gasp and a smack of his lips. He looked at me and winked as he set the shot glass down and said, "Man, I'm just a junk salesman, Martin. You know that. Whatever else I am, I can say it ain't my fault. My parents brought me up the only way they knew how, and if that was wrong, well, that's just too fucking bad. It's too late now, and I ain't crying about it."

"Product of your environment, you say."

He smacked his lips again and stroked his chin. "Momma always said, Son, you gotta pay for what you do. Strict Protestant fire-and-brimstone stuff. Church every Sunday, and during the week too, on special occasions. Back talk was good for a slap in the mouth. General infractions were good for a whupping with a belt. If I fucked up real good, she'd wait till Daddy came home, and he'd execute the punishment, whacking me with a belt or a Ping-Pong paddle. Don't get me wrong, Martin. I didn't enjoy it. But that's where I got the connection, you pay for what you do.

"This organist in church, she was mighty fine-looking to a young boy of ten. She was tall and prim and had the nicest, smoothest white skin you ever saw. Nice ass too, the way it spread out just slightly on the bench. Had a mole on the back of her neck, made you wanna bite it real hard. I used to sit there and watch her play and get a big old diamond cutter during church. I didn't really understand what sex was all about. I mean, I knew the actual mechanical way it worked and I knew it was highly recommended by everyone who tried it, but I didn't really know what it felt like. Didn't have a clue. I didn't know that doing it was gonna give me the satisfaction my young body craved. All I had was my imagination. So what come to mind was to strip this woman naked and tie her up. I'd tie her down to a board and stick pins in her. Spank her, put little clamps on her titties. Make her beg, and she'd love me for it. That's what I'd be thinking about during church, you know, watching that woman sitting on that organ bench playing those hymns so sweetly, me having a big old hard-on, not knowing what it was for."

"It's time to cut to the chase, Vick," I said. "This had better be leading up to something. Like a confession, I hope."

"Confession?" He feigned insult. "What do I have to confess about, Martin? You gotta get that outta your head. I haven't done nothing wrong. I don't know why I gotta keep telling you that. The things you're upset about ain't my fault, they're a whole different matter. I pay for what I do. I'm the godfather, I'm the rockin' daddy. You're on my turf here. You need some money, you come to me like you come to a bank. You go into a bank and say, I need some money. Then you wait for them to say, OK, we might be able to give you some money, and if you want to take it, here's the terms. That's what I do. I lay out the terms. You don't want to take them, fine. I'm not saying everybody has to have terms. There's plenty of people I just give stuff to, out of the goodness of my heart. I've given away a dozen guitars in the last ten years, no strings attached, so to speak, just here you go, play the shit out of it, boy. Clothes too. But if *you* come to *me,* you gotta be ready to let me dictate some terms. You understand what I'm saying?"

"I understand what I misunderstood before," I said. "I misunderstood that the reason you broke Donald Rollins's arm and then paid for it was because he owed you money and it was punishment for not paying you back. I misunderstood before that Leo got a guitar from you and a broken hand the same night but didn't realize the two were connected, two parts of one deal. You're sick, Vick. The kind of sickness you have may not be contagious, but it isn't good for the overall health of the community."

"Now hold on just a minute here," he said, his jowls shaking. "I don't hurt anybody, not really. You ain't as goddamn straight arrow as you think you are, I bet. Think about it: don't tell me when your girlfriend screams when you ram it in her it doesn't turn you on?"

"I don't want to hear this, Vick, I just want some facts."

"Well, look at it this way, Martin. I'm entitled to a little pleasure in this fucked-up world. Everybody has their little favorite things, and I got mine. If somebody's willing to accommodate me so that I can derive some enjoyment, where's the harm in that?"

"I told you, I want facts. Stop bullshitting around."

"Facts, shmacks," he drawled. "I like you, Martin. I don't know why, maybe because you remind me of dear old Momma. Always coming at me with some kinda angle, some kinda higher viewpoint. Hard-headed, old-fashioned. But I got the notion you're a modern enough guy to, uh, understand my position here. So hear me out, OK? You want a thousand bucks?"

"You owe me more than that," I said. I felt the hair on the back of my neck standing up, felt my face flushing, getting hot. "You lied to me, and our deal was that you weren't going to lie to me, or else you lose the shop."

"OK, two thousand," he said, trying to dismiss our contract with a shake of his head. "Plus, whatever you wanna know, I'll tell you. Consider this money an option fee, an option to negotiate. I guarantee, you hear me out, you're gonna see where I'm coming from, and you'll see I'm right. You interested?"

"You know what I'm interested in."

"OK, Martin. OK. Come on upstairs, then. It's cooler up there, and more comfortable, and it'll all make more sense up there."

He struggled to his feet and I followed him, with a mixture of dread and morbid curiosity, around the corner to a freight elevator. Ed the Head went up with us. I noticed that he'd picked up a black, rubber-gripped claw hammer from somewhere.

Vick's living quarters took up the second floor. It wasn't cooler, and it was mustier. The space ran the length of the building, unobstructed. Down both the lengthwise walls were windows that had been painted over a sickly green. Light came in from the street through the painted glass as a strange glow, illuminating the panes more than the room itself. It was as if the panes were radioactive, soaking up the light like cancerous cells. The furnishings were all rejects from the store—a sway-backed bed with a ragged homemade quilt and satin pillows with rust stains, a three-legged nightstand, and numerous sofas and recliners strewn haphazardly about like abandoned cars. A heavy butcher-block table as big as a grand piano was stationed just within reach of the bed, an ugly Tiffany lampshade suspended over it. Other than the creaking of the floor and the squeaking of the bedsprings as Vick tried to get comfortable, it was strangely quiet.

Ed was fondling the claw hammer and Vick was looking up at me half-lidded, with as much coyness as a 320-pound man wriggling out of a motorcycle jacket can muster. He was a bit red-faced and short of breath.

"I *like* you, Martin. And when I like somebody, I like to show it." He looked over at Ed, leaning against the butcher-block table, uncomfortably close to me, then his gaze rested on the hammer in Ed's hands. Great rolls of fat tumbled around underneath his undershirt as he swayed on the bed. "I like Leo, too. He needed a guitar, and I helped him out."

"This is making me sick, Vick. Why don't you just go ahead and say it?"

"OK, Martin. You think you're a pretty straight guy, right? Don't answer, 'cause I know it's true. And it's a fact, you are a helluva lot straighter than most. So I wouldn't bring you up here and try to buy you off cheap. You've heard that old proverb, about the guy who asks the gal if she'll fuck him for a million bucks. She says yes, for a million bucks I would. Then the guy asks her, How about for a hundred grand? How about for fifty bucks and a couple of drinks? She gets all insulted then and says, What do you think I am? And he says, We already established what you are, we're just haggling over the price."

"That's old as the hills, Vick."

"Sure, but it's as true as it ever was. It just so happens, in this proverb, pain is the thing. It's my thing. It gets me all excited in a way I can't explain. I don't know why. I just know it *excites* me. I tried doing things to myself, but it just don't work that way. If only pain wasn't so *painful*. But if someone else is willing to take it, *ooohh-ee*. A big shot of pleasure for me, just a little hurt for you, and a whole lotta money to help you forget about it. I bet you'd let me break your finger, any finger, or a toe, like maybe your big toe . . ."

Ed the Head brought out a pair of handcuffs from his jacket, grinning, wetting his lips with cruel anticipation. "It wouldn't hurt long, Martin," he said, reaching out, taking hold of the sleeve of my shaking arm.

"How 'bout ten thousand bucks, Martin? I'm rich now, man . . . *Twenty* thousand bucks. Huh, how about it? Could you turn it down?"

I jumped back from Ed, electrified, sucking in big gulps of air. Nausea rose in a tidal wave up from my gut, eating into my throat like battery acid, exploding into purple spots in front of my eyes. I reached back under my jacket and came out with the gun, holding it stiff-armed in both hands, first aiming at one, then the other.

Vick looked crestfallen. Ed the Head looked ready to pounce on me, jiggling the handcuffs in one hand, grinning, somewhat excited by my response. He laughed, an ugly, feral sound.

"DON'T FUCKING TOUCH ME," I yelled.

Vick's hand went up to his heart and he made a little cooing sound. "Oh, shit," he said, "I guess this means no."

"Damn right it means no, you goddamn freak."

"I shouldn't have offered you money. People think of it different when they do things for guitars, or leather jackets. I just thought since I have all this money . . ." He started to pout, then looked at me suspiciously. "I'm just trying to make a *point*, for chrissakes." He shook his head, keeping his eyes on the gun. "Jesus Christ, Martin, you aren't gonna shoot anybody."

He glanced at Ed, who wasn't laughing anymore, then back at me. Childishly, "Are you?"

After a while I settled down into just a slow, smoldering rage. I collapsed into a Naugahyde recliner held together by duct tape that stuck to my suit every time I moved. But I wasn't moving much, just sitting there, feeling the jaundiced glow from the green windowpanes as an encroaching symptom of the whole sick scenario. The gun was still in my hands, a heavy cold weight.

Vick was talking in a sort of singsong drawl.

"I mean, hell, it's not like I go out and attack people. I guarantee, you need the money bad enough, you'll be glad to do it. I mean, what I always say, if it's fun, people do it for free. That's what the whole principle of work is based on. So, in that sense, *lots* of guys have worked for me, people that'd surprise you. And it doesn't mean you're queer, for chrissakes. Leo sure as hell ain't. He didn't even scream when the hammer came down. I never hurt nobody—"

"Never hurt anybody?" I said. "What about Nadine, who can't even look at Leo anymore without crying?"

He shrugged his fat shoulders.

"What about Donald Rollins, comes to you for a beating so he can buy his last fix?"

Another shrug.

"And what about Retha Thomas?"

He didn't move. I looked at Ed, who was looking the other way. "What about Retha Thomas, you sonofabitch?"

He stayed still, just a blubbery iceberg with his lower lip sticking out. "Ask Eddie about that."

"I'm sick of hearing that," I said. "Whoever knows had better tell me. *Right now.*"

Ed the Head's face had cracked into an ugly grin. His eyes were hard marbles, unfocused, his lips curling out, baring his crooked teeth, as he said nonchalantly, "Weren't my fault the goddamn bitch . . ."

Vick cleared his throat and swatted the air with a shaky hand. "Retha had met this Brackenridge ER nurse down at the Goodwill store," he said. "The nurse told her about this kid who'd been down there a couple of times for broken toes. One of those times I did something stupid and paid him with a check, and he tried to get them to take his bill out of it. Well, it seemed like Retha was ready to run and tell the IMF guys about my little hobby here and I was afraid that'd blow my deal. I mean, maybe it wouldn't have five, ten years ago. But today, shit, just like that congressman who got run out on a rail 'cause he went to a rub joint a couple of times and got a gal pregnant. People act like a little fucking on the side is a capital crime nowadays, so I know they ain't gonna look kindly on me. They got Ted Bundy, they got AIDS, they got all kinds of things they can point to and say, See? I told you so, if it ain't normal it ain't right. So I gave Retha Thomas eight hundred bucks and some vintage jewelry as a little gift to keep her mouth shut. But Eddie's been asking for a raise, and he got his feelings hurt when he found out about it. So I said OK, whyn't you go get it back from her?"

Ed was grinning again. "I slipped her the Mickey at the party, but I didn't lay a finger on her."

"Expect her to have a car wreck?" I asked.

"Naw, I was just figuring to soften her up. Maybe I was pissed and just wanted to fuck her up, ruin her night. I didn't know she was with you at first. When you guys left I could see you weren't gonna be any good to her so I went back to her motel. When I got up to her room, somebody was inside, with the TV or radio going, so I split back to the party and ran into Leo."

"You expect me to believe that?"

He just shrugged. "I don't give a fuck if you do or not. But I wasn't gone long enough to do anything. Ask Leo, he'll—"

"Aw, shut up," I said. I looked over at Vick. "So Ed brought Leo over here and you had some sick fun with him and paid him with the Flying V?"

He nodded. I'd known it already, but having it confirmed

didn't make it go down any better. "Bingo visited Retha at the motel," I said. "She deposited another five hundred dollars in her account last week. You think it came from him?"

"I suppose," said Vick. "Stingy bastard, gave her less than I did. But why, you reckon?"

"She stumbled onto your secret, maybe she stumbled onto one of his. Maybe he tried to kill her because she wanted more money."

He shrugged. "Nah, he ain't like that, I don't think." He scratched his chin thoughtfully. "Well, maybe . . ."

"Have you paid him back the twenty thousand yet?"

"Fuck him. He ain't gonna get paid, neither."

"Why?"

"He's an asshole, that's why." He bounced on the bed, frowning, then reached for the Cuervo bottle and took a long drink.

"You don't seem too worried about it."

He just giggled. I looked away. Something caught my eye— a sliver of light peeking through one of the painted panes of glass where it was scratched. I heard Vick giggle again.

"You're not worried about being a big fat target for a doublebarrel shotgun?" I said.

"What do you mean?"

"I mean one of the guys who picked up the twenty thousand had one."

"I still don't get you."

"I mean, you don't seem to be scared of a guy you have every reason in the world to be scared of. He's a guy who's not known as a big fountain of patience and goodwill, yet here you are, going around to Antone's with money just flying out of your wallet, buying drinks for people, and he hasn't asked you to pay it back yet."

"Way I recall it, you didn't tell him exactly when I'd be able to," he said.

"Don't bullshit me, Vick."

"You're the one blowing smoke up my ass. You got something to say, whyn't you go on and say it?"

"OK," I said. "I'm saying that Bingo hasn't asked for the repayment of your loan yet because it was him who hit you up for the twenty grand to begin with. I'm saying it was a dry run. I'm saying that he knew you were getting the hundred grand. That's what he wants, and he thinks he can get it."

"You saying it was all a ruse, to set me up for when I *did* have the cash, to see if I was ripe for blackmail?"

"I know it was, you know it was, and you know I know it was. First, it was too easy to talk him into loaning it to you, a guy he hasn't spoken to for three years. Then, he plays ignorant about how well your artists have been doing, and one thing Bingo Torres is not, is ignorant. But what really gives you away is the fact that after you get the money from the record deal, you don't seem to be too worried about paying him back, because you know he's not really out any money."

"Well, I didn't know—"

"To hell with you, you knew."

There was a sound, like a car door being shut. Ed went over to the window, peering down through a cracked pane. He said, "Why don't we ask him? He and Roberto are walking up to the front door now."

"Fuck him," said Vick. "Fuck him and his twenty grand blackmail bullshit."

"Roberto has an ax handle," said Ed. "We might as well let them in or they'll smash the door."

Vick put one hand on his heart and the other on the Cuervo bottle, saying, "Oh, Lord, move over. Fat man coming through."

We went back down to the guitar room while Ed let Bingo and Roberto in and led them back. Bingo looked around disdainfully, as if he were trying to determine the source of a bad smell. Roberto stood at his side, tapping his palm with the ax handle. Bingo polished the nails of his right hand on his lapel, then rested both hands on his hips.

"Well, Martin," he said, "your girlfriend from LA is hanging in there. Who knows, she might pull through."

"You'd better hope so," I said.

"I didn't touch her," he countered, indignant. "She called me and told me strange stories that she heard around town. She told me she was going to testify in court that I was friends with this *puto,* this pervert with his nasty little hobby," he spat. "And that would embarrass my family. It would also make my lawyers very unhappy. But . . . that's not what we're here to discuss, if you don't mind, Martin." He shot a glance at Roberto, who stopped tapping the ax handle in midstroke.

My back was against the window and Vick and Ed were more or less in the corner by the office door. Vick sat on a square red Marshall speaker cabinet. Light from the waning moon poured in over my shoulders, getting soaked up by the whites of Bingo Torres's eyes and his white linen suit. Roberto wore the same electric blue suit, black shirt, and turquoise necklace, and I was thinking back on how I'd thought of him as a caricature of a '50s East Side low-rider tough guy. But now he was a caricature with an ax handle, and that was a whole other matter. They would also both have guns and knives, but Bingo was too classy to walk around with his out unless he deemed it absolutely necessary. Or if he was in the mood. The rack of hanging guitars at their backs made strange shadows on the back wall, looming large and elongated, like hanged men.

Bingo extended his arms, drinking in the moonlight, addressing us like a CEO at a board meeting. "That is not what we are here to discuss. We aren't even here to discuss anything, we are here to collect." Roberto's ax handle came down on the guitar display, hard, and wood cracked. "We are here to collect money."

"Fuck you, Bingo," said Vick. "Fuck you and your twenty grand bullshit."

Bingo laughed. "I had to know you were ready to pay. You must have felt just a little bit of guilt, didn't you, making all this money because of records I paid for, you perverted asshole."

Vick snorted. "Whyn't you cut your own deal with a major label, then, you think you're entitled to it? Instead of trying to cut yourself in on this thing."

Bingo puffed out his chest and sneered. "Because, it's not a good time for me to have a big profile in the music industry. And, I am not after the twenty thousand dollars. I want all of it."

"You're outta your mind," said Vick.

"All of it," repeated Bingo. "I know you've got it here, or close by. You never did like banks, did you, Victor? Too bad for you, convenient for me. Are you going to give it to me, or do I let Roberto give you a taste of your own medicine?"

Roberto was ready, stepping forward, ready to swing at Vick. Vick cowered, wheezing, and Ed looked ready to do something, no one knew what. I cleared my throat, lightened my waistband, and came up with the 9 mm.

"It's cocked," I said, "and I'm pissed."

"You wouldn't shoot me," said Bingo, laughing sardonically.

"You'll sound funny trying to repeat that with your lips stitched shut and your veins full of embalming fluid," I said.

I must have sounded convincing, because after a minute of hard glares and some spitting on the floor near Vick, they walked backward out of the store, got in the black Mercedes, and peeled out.

## 22

"YOU LIED TO ME, YOU SONOFABITCH," I screamed. "You lied to me, you lied to me, and I told you that you better not lie."

Ed the Head looked bored, lurking again, rolling his dark marble eyes under his concrete brow. Vick lay nearly prostrate on the speaker cabinet, staring up at the ceiling, sweating buckets, breathing heavily.

"You knew Bingo was fucking with you and you used me to fuck with him back. You knew Retha Thomas was ready to talk about your little hobby with anybody who would listen, with the people who are prosecuting Bingo and with the IMF crowd too. You bought her silence with a measly eight hundred dollars and didn't bother to tell her that Bingo wouldn't be so easy to deal with."

"I think I'm gonna have a heart attack, Martin. Don't be hassling me like this. I'm a living time bomb."

Ed scuffed along the wall, staring out the window, running his hand down the long ledge, stirring up the dust he'd neglected on his cleanups.

"This means I get the store, you know," I said, realizing how petty it sounded. I kicked a speaker cabinet so hard it tumbled over. Vick whimpered with shock.

"I really think I could stuff both of you in a trash dumpster and set it on fire and not look back or lose any sleep. The whole reason I've sullied myself with you two is that I wanted to know what happened to Retha Thomas. I had this feeling that you tried to kill her, or got someone else to do it, or knew who did. I had this feeling that I could find out if I just kept digging away at the manure pile of your existence. But what do I find out? You guys didn't do it, or you say you didn't do it, and I half-ass believe you because none of you sincerely seem to give a good goddamn about her one way or the other. Ed the Head tried to poison her with one of his goddamn elephant downers and he even fucked that up. Bingo hates your guts on principle and wants your money because he thinks you sort of owe it to him and because he thinks you're so despicable that he's entitled to it anyway, like the neighborhood bully taking away a wimp's lunch money."

"Whyn't you just lay off?" droned Ed.

"I really feel bad, Martin," said Vick between gasps and burping sounds. "I think I might have a bleeding ulcer, too."

"I sure as hell hope you do, and I hope you're enjoying the pain," I said. "Somehow you two clowns are responsible for this whole mountain of shit, even though your denial-addled brains can't admit it. You and your little hobby that supposedly doesn't hurt anybody—look what happened to Retha. Look what happened to Leo, look what happened to Donald Rollins."

"That wasn't our fault, man," said Ed, suddenly a chatterbox.

"SHUT THE FUCK UP!" I shouted. "I don't ever want to hear those words from you two assholes again. You got me?"

Ed shrugged. Vick let out a raspy, phlegmatic sigh.

"Nobody ever wants to accept any responsibility in this town for anything," I said. "No wonder nothing ever gets done around here, this is the laziest fucking town in the world. *It's not my fault . . . It's not my job . . . It's not a good day for me, I'm going down to Barton Springs to go swimming . . .* Someday the sun will decide it's not its responsibility to rise here, and you'll all fucking freeze to death. But you'll die in bed because you'll keep waiting for noon to come before you get up."

They weren't even listening. I didn't even care.

"You think they'll come back, with guns?" said Ed.

I leaned my face against the window, feeling the cool glass, pressing it harder till the nerves didn't register the temperature, only the pain. "I don't know," I said.

At four-thirty they called. Bingo asked to talk to me. When I took the phone, a female voice said, "Martin—" Then, nothing but screams. It was Barbra Quiero.

"You like this cunt?" said Bingo over the screaming.

"Don't you dare—"

"You like her or a hundred grand better?"

"I like her," I said. "I want her to live."

"Drive out toward my house with the money in an hour or I'll kill the cunt."

"I'll do it."

"Good boy. She won't be here, so don't get any ideas. Somebody'll stop you on the road and make the swap. Oh, I almost forgot. You know, we didn't leave Vick's empty-handed. Can you see your car from where you are?"

"No . . ."

"Well, you'll find out. You'll find out especially if you don't bring the money. You'll get a very bad reputation with your instruments, Martin."

He hung up. The son of a bitch had my bass guitar and he was going to beat her to death with it.

"I'm not going to argue," I said. They looked at me like I was the one who was crazy. "Where's the money?"

"It ain't here," said Vick.

"Bullshit. You've been practically waving it in Bingo's face, taunting him with it, throwing it around at the club, and he seems to know you well enough that he knew it would be here. So don't lie to me."

Vick roused himself just slightly, propping himself up on one elbow. His face was mottled, dripping sweat. He smelled bad. His hands shook, and the blubber that rolled over his belt jiggled like Jell-O. "Look, Martin, whyn't we try and wait him out, see what happens? Maybe I could call him back, try to reason . . ."

I cocked the gun.

"Fuck her," said Ed. "I don't know this chick, don't know anybody around here who fits that description. You, Vick?"

Vick didn't answer. He knew I wouldn't back down.

"The money," I said. "Where is it?"

"Uh-uh," grunted Ed. "Ain't no way—"

"Aw, Eddie," whined Vick, "I think we got to go along with him. Maybe we can get it back after he gets the girl. We'll call the cops after. They'll help us get it back. It's our money, goddamn it. It ain't like it's drug money."

Ed grunted again. I moved up and let him see me flick the safety button off the "safe" position.

"*Eeeeddd-dddeeeEEEEEE?*" pleaded Vick, trying to muster a tremulous imitation of authority in his shaky voice. "We *will* go to the cops after, OK?" His tone was singsongy, like he was talking to a small child. "I can fix things, Eddie. They know me down there."

"Come on, Vick," I said. "We don't have all night."

"It's in the lock box in the office, Martin," he sighed, "but Eddie has the key."

Ed growled, baring his teeth in an animalistic smile, backing away against the guitar rack. A couple of vintage six-strings rocked as he bumped into them, causing the shadows that had reminded me of hanged men to dance wildly back and forth.

"Come on, Head, be a good boy," I said.

A thin line of spit ran out of the corner of his grinning mouth. He ripped open his shirt, the buttons scattering on the floor. The key was on a chain around his neck, hanging down in front of his hairless chest. He started to laugh. That ugly sound.

Vick pleaded, "Eddie . . ."

But the tuxedoed caveman spun on his heels and ran out of the room. I raised the gun, thought better, jammed it down my pants, and tore after him. By the time I cleared the first row of coat racks, I heard a crash and then the sound of a shower of shattering glass colliding with itself and the sidewalk. Ed the Head had run through the glass door.

I took off after him. He was headed down the sidewalk at a dead run. I followed, past the Sheraton Crest parking garage, then the hotel itself, cutting through the drive past the lobby, past a couple of idling tour buses, into the crosswalk of Congress Avenue just before the bridge.

My shoes, a pair of vintage Stacy Adams two-tone wing tips, were great for standing behind a bass guitar but not for running, and they were cutting into my feet. I tasted blood in my mouth and hot sharp pains in my throat as I dodged the traffic. My lungs ached and I fully expected that they would come flying out of my mouth on my next labored breath, bloody, inside out, dripping cigarette tar. He cut left on the other side, nearly hitting a flattop kid on a ten-speed mountain bike, and took off across the bridge. When I got to the other side he still had a good thirty yards on me and the kid on his bike had stopped, staring open-mouthed at the two of us. I said I was sorry and knocked him off and hopped on. He was too young to be out so late anyway.

I pumped the cranks hard, bearing down, feeling the pull of the dark waters below. A couple of cars breezed past, making ghostlike sounds. A truck went by, too, causing the bridge to shake, reminding me that I did not want to tumble over the rail. On the bike it didn't take me long to catch up with Ed. When I was no more than ten yards behind him, he turned and saw me and slowed to a stop. I hopped off the bike and let it roll out onto the pavement.

He stood there, his shirt open, the chain dangling on his hairless chest. His legs were spread apart, his gnarled hands open, the fingers gesticulating like disturbed maggots. I stepped closer and pulled the gun. When he saw it he stepped up on the railing and teetered there, taunting me, fingering the chain around his neck.

"Come on, asshole, shoot me," he beckoned.

I inched forward. He grinned, flicking the key with one finger so it would dance off his chest, and he started screaming "COME ON MOTHERFUCKER COME ON" and laughing, his big wide monkey mouth cracking open his skull, that ugly sound hacking forth from it.

He sounded like a bad dog barking.

I could shoot him and he'd fall off the bridge into the lake with the key still around his neck, or we could fight. So I jammed the gun back in my pants and closed in, ready to tangle. He hopped down off the railing as soon as I came within striking distance and we went to it.

It was a weird dance, feinting blows, dodging cars that came too close, trying to avoid slipping over the railing. He was quick and kept his fists up close to his temples like a boxer, blocking my jabs. I took a couple in the face once, and instead of ducking completely out of reach I kneed him in the groin. He connected solidly on my left side but I locked my arms around him and pulled him down. I was heavier than him and we hit the concrete hard. I felt the wind go out of him. He struggled like a wild animal, clawing and kicking, but I clapped his right ear and gave him a tooth-rattling right and then backhanded him. While he was still dazed I went for the key chain. But as I was slipping it off he nodded back and smashed my hand between his head and the pavement, then got a knee between my legs and wedged me off. By the time I got up on all fours he was dancing in front of me again, drooling blood and spit. First I saw him dangling the key off the side of the bridge, then I saw the sole of his shoe flash up. It sent me reeling backward like a rug had been pulled out from under my feet.

That blow shot a new dose of adrenaline into my system, or maybe it was the blood I tasted. I scrambled to my feet and went after him with renewed fury, plowing into him with my head low. He went limp, his arms curling around me like a dead-drunk dancing partner. I found the chain entwined in my fingers and snatched it and slipped it over my head. For good measure I kneed him in the groin before I reached for my gun. Once I had the key, he wasn't going to get it back. I didn't care if I had to shoot him now or not.

But somehow he locked a calf behind one of my legs and grabbed my belt and yanked, and the next thing I knew we were on the wrong side of the rail.

The world shifted in an instant. The night tilted and we spilled out of it. There was nothing between me and the earth but the cool mossy air thick with bat wings freight-training by as I sailed off the bridge, down to the dark waters below.

It wasn't like flying, it wasn't oblivion. It was being fried in bug juice, it was one long scream that turned inside out in my throat. I hit the water like a ton of bricks. Blackness. Coldness. Down, sucked down. Swirling currents, slimy, serpentine things caressing me, slick as vomit. Gargling sounds in my head. Open your eyes, a voice said. I opened them but it did no good; no way was up. A school of carp as big as dogs scraped past me, and still I tumbled. It took an eternity and it took no time at all. When I popped back up on the surface, it seemed I'd plunged down through the cold murk forever. Then it seemed like it had been only a second, or like a bad dream that hadn't happened at all. Had I blacked out? It didn't matter as I choked and saw red and gurgled and thrashed and belched water. I was too panicked to be scared. I was dead already.

I'm a poor swimmer.

I sank down again, fought, surfaced again. A bat swooped down, shrieked, disappeared. Two black snakes spermed out of nowhere like black lightning. Somewhere in the dark cave of my brain, Logic clawed at Panic. Panic said fuck off, not now. But arms and legs had found a rhythm in the meantime, found a stroke that held the bottom-crawling monsters of the lake just out of tentacles' reach. Realizing that somehow, some part of me was trying to save the rest of me, I gained a few inches against Panic and summoned up a Voice. It came on strong, roaring with authority, like a high school coach, like an old-time revivalist preacher, as full of fire as a hell-bent rock and roller.

Do it, it said. You have a choice, a chance, a free throw in the game against death. Take it. *Fight.*

I fought.

No way you want to taste the nasty water down there again, said the Voice, and it was right. I would swallow more—I knew that—but tasting it on the surface with the bat-flecked sky above was one thing, tasting it in terror with the awful vegetation tickling my feet and the liquid darkness all around was quite another. I knew if I went down again I probably wouldn't come back up. Not for a couple of days, anyway. I sucked in as much of the mossy air as I could and managed to hold on to the surface for a while longer, still fighting, still hearing that voice. Kick that lake in the balls, boy, it said.

Around that time I suddenly became aware of a jolting sensation in my right arm as I struggled with the water. It seemed to happen with every stroke as I arced my arms outward, and there was a muffled, gargled explosive sound, too. Then I figured it out—I was still holding on to the gun, and I was shooting the damn lake. I stuck it in the pocket of my jacket. I immediately regretted it, too. The weight banging against my hip as I wrestled the water seemed like a fatal mistake, but I wasn't going to stop treading water again to take it out of the pocket and discard it.

The current had carried me under the bridge and past it to the east, toward Longhorn Dam. Above me, a soupy sky with no stars. On the south bank, the Austin American-Statesman building was just barely visible, obscured by a weedy no-man's-land of transients' plastic garbage bag tents and flickering campfires. On the north side, I couldn't avoid noticing the red glow of the Sheraton Crest sign, several of the letters burned out, making it read "herat rest," which I did not want for an epitaph, but the hotel was soon upstream from me. And the lights were still on at Vick's Vintage. There I was, in sight of the place, drowning, and the money was there, and Barbra was about to be murdered, if it wasn't too late already. I'd come a long way down since spending all afternoon and last night, newly cleansed of guilt, in the arms of my angel. Now I knew nearly the whole dark truth, and it was sucking me the rest of the way under.

I never saw Ed the Head after we hit the water.

My arms were getting tired, and I was starting to swallow more and more water. I saw more snakes. The Voice began to fade, and I faded with it. I began to see less and less of the banks and skyline and soupy overhead as my will wore down. So heavy, so tired. The water didn't taste so bad after all.

But for a little longer I kicked and flapped my arms and

gulped air, not bothering to fight the current, not thinking of Lasko or Ed the Head or Barbra or Bingo. Maybe I thought of them a little. Maybe I was thinking of Retha, how if I died now she would probably die too and that would be my fault. Maybe I was thinking of Ladonna, and how unfair it would be for me to die without getting to say the things I should have said, without putting everything just right. Maybe I was thinking of Leo, how he could get past what he'd done, if he just tried. Look at me, I thought, I'm trying to keep afloat, and it's hard as hell. Nothing you do in life is harder than not dying. Nothing. And once you've got that licked, even temporarily, you can lick anything. You've got to try. It's your responsibility. Because other people can't even keep from dying, the cards are so stacked against them. They're unlucky. We aren't. We were born lucky.

But it felt like my luck was running out. I started thinking I was some kind of lake creature, nocturnal, reptilian. Some kind of slimy refugee from an oil slick Antarctica. My world was nothing but gurgles and slime and crickets. My limbs were numb, my extremities evaporating, evolving. I was the last of a strange breed. Current was taking me somewhere, someplace it had in mind for me to go. I fought to keep my eyes open and my muscles working for just a little while longer and suddenly there it was: something white, glowing surreally on the surface, dancing subtly, like the gently moving wings of a hovering angel.

Like a dream, we came together, but each time I tried to grab her, she shot out from my grasp. Some of my will returned and I managed to get one arm around her, but still she fought. Lighter than I'd imagined an angel would be, and somewhat unyielding to my embrace, she bucked and bobbed underneath me, carrying both of us along. I made no promise to be gentle as I mounted her, skin actually squeaking as I dug my nails deeper. The lake seemed to move faster underneath us during the struggle. But I held her cheek to cheek and my eyes were filled with the whiteness of her skin, painfully aware of the dark universe above and below.

Alive. There we were, after a nap, lying spent, side by side in a gooey bed of weeds and black mush. I opened my eyes and reached for a cigarette, extracted the memorial Camel pack from my jacket and dug out a wet wad of paper and tobacco and flung it on her, realizing how out of it I was, seeing that she had turned into a coffin, rocking rhythmically in the weeds. Six feet long and two feet deep and a yard wide, with the name MCPHAIL FLORIST AND GREENHOUSE on the side, she was a Styrofoam flower shipping container. She squeaked as I let my other arm fall off her to pull something out of my hair. A star winked overhead. I tried to focus on it, but it avoided my gaze, preferring instead to hover in a blurry circular pattern. A column of bats swarmed up from the southern shore and spiraled across the lake like a column of cinders from a large fire, squeaking like rusty bedsprings.

Slowly—it seemed like hours—I got to my knees. Everything still moved with wavelike motion, and I could still feel the pull of the river, trying to tug me farther downstream, farther east, over the dam.

Crawling wasn't so bad. It was better than squirming and wriggling and drowning. The bank was slippery, almost impossible, but I clawed my way up it and rolled over on a grass embankment. Solid ground. Good. The grass didn't seem to move underneath me, and the winking star overhead gradually stopped going in circles. I felt that withered morning-after feeling as I crawled up the rise to the street. I had the ragged, sick sensation that I'd run through a party naked, and now it was time to go home.

It took another couple of years to get to my feet, but once I did, they worked OK. The feet were encased in solid black muck and they moved across the grassy expanse behind a construction site. A route between buildings led out to a street, and it was still 1st Street, the right side of the lake, thankfully, where one foot went in front of the other, squish, squash, until gradually, the feet were once again, although somewhat tenuously, connected to a brain. The gun banged against my thigh like a hard tumor. I felt around my neck. The key chain was still there. I began to run. Down one last long block to the thrift shop, up the sidewalk, through the glass door that wasn't there anymore. I could still smell the sweet green smell from the wet grave as I stumbled toward the back of the store.

Vick came out of the office and looked at me in abject horror. His mouth dropped open, his belly shook. "Wha? Oh, my God. Where's Eddie?"

I gave him a look that was as chilly as I felt, as chilly as the dripping gun I stuck under his nose, and he didn't ask any more questions, just grabbed the key out of my hands and ran back to the safe in the office. I got the money and blurred out of there.

The sound of screeching tires ricocheted around the streets as the Ghia careened around corners. There was a yellow blur through red lights, a lake in a rearview mirror.

24

The trip was both nightmarishly long and surreally short. Every dot of the dotted lines on the road was a heartbeat, but my heart was beating very fast. My mental faculties had begun checking back in one by one, like tardy students. I'd have to play it by ear, I'd have to play tough. He wouldn't really want to kill the girl, would he? But how would he be able to deny charges by Vick, Barbra, and me that he kidnapped her and we paid ransom unless—

Unless everybody was dead.

I put that thought out of my mind and concentrated only on the road, the rippling ribbon of asphalt rolling under my wheels. I felt the sideways pull of the curves, the displacement of gravity as I sailed over the hills into the blackness.

Where would they flag me down? Somewhere past the loop, I reasoned, since there were other ways to get to Ranch Road 2222. Just a few miles past it, up a steep hill, then around that harrowing curve with the breathtaking view was Bingo's house. I chewed up the miles, and finally just ahead, at the crest of the hill, there was a shape.

It turned out to be a Mercedes station wagon. Two figures walked out to the middle of the road and pointed flashlights at me, signaling for me to pull off the road next to them. I slowed down and eased off the shoulder into tall dry grass. The figures turned out to be Roberto and his nameless companion. Both had double-barrel shotguns as well as flashlights.

"Toss your gun out of the car," said Roberto.

Out it went.

He walked over, pausing to pick it up, leading with the shotgun. The feel of my cold, wet gun in his hand elicited only a curled lip. As he came alongside he said, "Let's see the money."

I held open the Safeway bag with what was left of the $100,000 after Vick had been to Antone's. Roberto gave Nameless the OK sign, then came around to the passenger side and got in, curling his lip again at my appearance. "You're late," he said. "We better get a move on."

"To Bingo's?" I asked.

When he nodded, I decided that all the witnesses who weren't on Bingo's team were most likely not going to see the sun come up again. And by my estimation, it was nearly six o'clock. Not long to live.

I begged for a cigarette.

A car that looked like Barbra Quiero's Mercedes was in the drive when we pulled up. The station wagon stopped just short of the drive and flashed its high beams three times. Afterwards, a figure got out of the passenger side of the Mercedes and put his black cowboy hat back on his head as the car backed up and pulled out onto the road and sped away.

The driver had looked like Barbra Quiero. It had to be, I reasoned. Well, Bingo had lied when he said she wouldn't be out at the house, but at least they had let her go. The figure with the black cowboy hat turned out to be Bingo. He motioned for the station wagon to park in front and for me to pull in beside it.

We went inside. Nameless led the way, I carried the money, and Roberto tried to fuse a couple of my vertebrae with the shotgun barrels.

Bingo wrinkled his nose, looking over the pile of paper money as Roberto stacked and counted it, sorting out the counted stacks on one side of the shotgun lying across the long heavy oak dining table. "What the hell happened to you?" he asked. I had tracked in mud over the Navaho rugs and I was still dripping. At least he didn't have to worry about me scuffing the floor. I didn't have any shoes.

"Ed the Head and I went for a swim," I said. "I didn't have time to shower off before coming out, and I guess Ed was going to wash up on shore."

He gave me a blank look, then almost laughed, slapping Roberto on the back, then going around the end of the table to sit down across from me. "That's what they call gallows humor, isn't it, Martin?"

"Except it's not a gallows I have to worry about, is it?"

He shook his head slowly, pushing a liter bottle of Absolut over to my side, motioning for me to sit down. Roberto slid a chair against my legs. "Drink up, Martin. I insist."

I plopped down in the chair. Squish. Roberto gave me a little elbow room and went back to counting the money. He slipped a rubber band around a stack, wrote down a figure on a notepad, and started packing it all in a briefcase. Nameless wasn't in sight, but I could hear him moving things around in an adjacent room.

The interior of the house was totally committed to Southwestern style, with lots of pink and white and various desert tones, desert textures, saltillo tile, Navaho rugs, rawhide-backed chairs. The dining area was high-ceilinged and looked out on a cactus garden on one end. There was a fireplace made of local limestone at my back and a wet bar with gold fixtures and a granite backsplash in one corner. Right out of *Texas Monthly,* except for the Danelectro case against the wall, which would be too hip for them. On the wall just over Bingo's head was a glass-framed watercolor of a cow skull and cactus garlanded with marigolds.

"You seem like you're in a hurry, Bingo. Got a plane to catch?"

He giggled. "As a matter of fact, I do. I don't think I can stick around for this payola thing. Such a trial would result in a lot of time indoors for Bingo, and Bingo doesn't like to be cooped up indoors like a mushroom. You see, Victor and his disgusting little hobby complicates things. It attracts things like that girl, Retha Thomas, snooping around, then she gets herself hurt real bad," he said, knitting his eyebrows to show his distaste. "You see? It makes it very uncomfortable for me, since, as you can guess, I have other interests besides record promotion that are not, uh, as they say, completely legal? They are a little bit illegal, and like they say, you can't be just a little bit pregnant, and you can't be a little bit dead. So you, you have stumbled into this thing and I really am sorry, but the minute you stumbled into it you became a little bit dead. Now we have to help you get all the way, and I was wondering, Martin, would you rather get too drunk and fall in the lake and drown, or would you rather get too drunk and drive your Karmann Ghia off this mountain out here?"

"Let me have a drink and think about it," I said. I took a big two-handed drink. There was no other way to do it. Roberto had tied my hands.

"Victor," said Bingo, rocking back in his chair, "is going to have a heart attack. You know why?"

"Why?"

"Because he's a fat tub of shit with nothing to lose if he testifies against me," he spat, slamming his fist down on the table. Roberto looked up, grinned, and went back to shuffling papers. There were big stacks of them, and he was having trouble arranging them in a large black leather carry-on bag. The briefcase was full. Roberto's shotgun lay next to it, a few inches from Bingo's drumming fingertips, but a long way from my tied hands. I eased my chair back a few inches. The legs made a barking sound on the tile.

"You're going to help him have this heart attack, aren't you?" I said.

He nodded. "A guy . . . I got a guy that's down there now. He's going to tell Vick he's going to cut his balls off. But don't worry. Vick will have a heart attack before he gets his zipper down."

"Why go to all this trouble for a measly hundred grand, Bingo? Seems like you'd have ten times that much stashed away for a quick trip south."

He jutted his jaw out defiantly and said, "It's no trouble, really. The money isn't much, this is true. But it's *my money*. I paid for those records to be made, so I deserve the money. Victor doesn't deserve anything but a quick *adiós*."

I took another drink, and that seemed to please him. It didn't seem to have any effect on me.

Bingo leaned back in his chair again, balancing himself as he talked, stretching his neck muscles out, rolling his eyes. I tried to imagine him dangling at the end of a rope, a noose cutting into the smooth brown flesh around his throat. "Fat people disgust me," he said. "You, Martin, come on, drink up . . . I don't have any reason to like you. But at least you look like a human being, not some big mountain of lard. I could forgive Victor's nasty little proclivities when he looked like a man, but when I think of him, little fat dick folded up against his blubber, wanking off at the thought of torturing boys, oh, it makes me sick. Drink up, Martin. I don't have much time. Roberto could hurry you up, you know."

Roberto tapped another stack of papers on the table, paused to look at the shotgun, then over at me.

I picked up the bottle again, took a long drink, letting the liquid gurgle, knowing that I had to do something, even if it was incredibly stupid, because soon the vodka would have an effect. So it wasn't altogether faked when the bottle wobbled in my hands as I took it from my mouth. But when I reestablished my grip around the neck of the bottle I raised it over my head and walloped Bingo in the face as hard as I could.

He went over backward, grabbing for Roberto's shotgun, and

I scrambled over the table after him. The shotgun clattered to the floor as I went all the way over, down on top of him. The chair folded into kindling wood under our combined weight, and the fall freed my wrists from their bonds. Bingo had a lot of the fight knocked out of him, at least temporarily, and I had already gained a strange, if uncomfortable, advantage by the time I heard Roberto unsnap a holster and cock a pistol. I adjusted my position and saw him as he stepped back and crouched down, but after I smashed the bottle against the clay tile and jabbed a pointed edge against his employer's jugular, there wasn't much he could do.

But Nameless came into the room blasting. His first barrel of buckshot blasted plaster and glass off the wall over our heads, destroying the cactus and cow skull watercolor. Bingo panicked as a long shard of glass from the painting stuck in his eye. Breaking free of my hold, he howled something in Spanish and bolted upright, just as Nameless's shotgun thundered again. Blood rained. He fell.

"*Dios mío*," cried Nameless. "Jefe, forgive me!"

But El Jefe wasn't in a forgiving mood. His heart had been strained through the back of his rib cage.

I struggled to wrench myself out from under the twitching body, able to see only Nameless's spastic leg movement from my position as he reloaded the double barrel. I couldn't see Roberto, but I heard the crack-crack-crack as his bullets started flying. I felt a hard lump between my body and Bingo's and realized it was Roberto's shotgun just as Nameless fired his again, powdering the tile floor where Bingo's hand had been when it was still attached to his arm. I blew what must have been parts of it out of my mouth and wrenched the shotgun out from under Bingo's body and quickly squeezed off a round toward my left, where it sounded like Roberto's pistol shots were coming from. There was a crashing sound and I saw his blue suit as he tumbled down, minus parts of both kneecaps. Nameless cried out in Spanish and his shotgun took a bite out of a table leg and the floor. I blasted again and crawled away a few feet to the end of the table, looking for a way out, then heard the clacking of leather soles on the clay tile. I risked peeking over the table top. Roberto was screaming in anguish, rolling a bloody pattern on the floor, peppering the stucco walls with lead.

"*Dios mío,*" echoed Nameless's voice again as his clacking feet took him out of the house.

And I rolled out from under the table just in time to see him hit the front door at a dead run. Seconds later a Mercedes engine turned over, gravel flew, and rubber melted on pavement.

I dove out the back door, piled into the Ghia, and peeled out through the same cloud of smoke and dust he'd left in. The wrenching curves that could pull you apart at forty miles an hour, I took at fifty-five. Down the hill past where I'd been stopped, off into the gravel, back again. I couldn't hear his engine or hear his screeching wheels but I flew through his dust shortly after he'd made it and I breathed his smoke just after he belched it and I could feel the rumble of his engine and I knew I would get him. I knew I would get him.

Just atop the crest of the next rise, through the raw V that the road had been laid into, the sun was setting fire to the hills in the east, just this side of town. The sky was turning a battleship gray and somewhere out there, I was sure, birds were starting to sing. But the next song I heard was that of screeching tires and impacting metal and flying glass. I braked and downshifted and got a shocking surprise as I topped the hill.

Just on the other side was a roadblock of blue and whites and a couple of sheriff's department vehicles. The Mercedes station wagon had taken out quite a bit of the midsection of one of them. I stood on the brake and did my best to correct the skid and still ended up in the ditch, window-deep in Johnson grass, choking from dust.

I got the door open and tumbled out. I heard feet coming toward me and in back of them, nearer the roadblock, a shout. Then another, and a whooping sound. "Whooee," hollered a booming voice. "Sumbitch made it through the roadblock. Car didn't, but he sure as shit did. Reyes—radio EMS and tell 'em to brang a putty knife." I knew they were talking about Nameless. Now he would get to tell Bingo he was sorry again. Face to face, more or less.

As I hoisted myself upright, other voices told me to freeze. Uniforms, uniforms with guns—their eyes bugged out as I emerged from the ditch. One of them started laughing, the other flicked out his handcuffs. Then another voice boomed out in the crisp early morning air, "Hold on, hold on just a second. That's Fender."

I welcomed that voice. It was Lasko's. I staggered out to the middle of the road and looked toward the tangled mass of metal that had been the station wagon, looking like it was trying to burrow into the patrol car. Twenty yards past the roadblock a headless bundle of clothing and entrails twitched on the pavement.

There was a fragment of reflective glass in the road down by my feet and I looked at it, a sliver of a hole going down into the center of the earth. Staring back up at me from the depths was a monster. Green-black spikes jutting out from a head that was mostly black, now cracking and dry but covered with red pinpoints of blood, clothing daubed with green and black muck encasing a body that swayed, patches of it shimmering and red-tinged, dripping with Bingo Torres's life fluid. No shoes. That monster was me.

"Godawmighty," said Lasko. "Godawmighty Jesus."

I told Lasko most of my end of the story on the way back to town, and he told me his. Vick had phoned the police right after I left with the ransom money, so they managed to run right into Bingo's cowboys as they dropped over to perform the radical vasectomy. I just hoped that they hadn't already been over to the Radisson. Sure, they'd apparently let her go, but that didn't mean that someone wasn't waiting there for her when she returned. And by now I was sure as hell that she hadn't merely been paranoid when she said she was being followed.

"Just relax, Martin," said Lasko as we got back to town. "She's either OK or she ain't. We find out when we get there."

"What were you doing out there on the roadblock, anyway? I thought this wasn't your case anymore."

"Martin," he growled affectionately, "get real. I hear this shit on the radio coming down, wild horses ain't gonna keep me away."

We pulled up in the hotel drive right behind a big black limo. A uniformed cop came over to Lasko's window and nodded hello. "It's OK," the cop said. "She's in there alone, and we've got men posted in the halls, too. But Watson just radioed and said—"

Lasko shushed him and nodded at me to go on up alone. "Thanks," I said. "She doesn't have any reason to trust anyone else. Just give me a minute."

The bell captain and the desk clerks turned white as I padded into the lobby. I showed them my key and told them to send up some more towels, chop chop.

The hall was quiet as I got off the elevator. Most of the rooms had DO NOT DISTURB signs hung on the doors. I was shaking from head to toe. The cops stationed by the exits squinted their eyes hard upon seeing me, then spoke discreetly into walkie-talkies and eventually let me pass.

She didn't answer my knock. As I put the key in the door and let myself in I heard water running. The bathroom door was partially shut and there were two suitcases parked at the foot of the bed, two airline tickets by the telephone.

The water stopped and she called out. Her voice was vibrant, just a bit tremulous and sweet with bathroom reverb. She said, "Bingo, is that you?"

I didn't say a word, just listened to a big bass drum of a heart. Thunk, thunk. She called out again, those red artificial nails appearing on the edge of the door as it slowly swung open and she leaned out, her back turned toward me, wet and naked, the mellow dark color of her skin uninterrupted by tan lines.

"Daddy, is that you?"

After I answered, she spun around quickly, reeling as if she'd been struck. She turned and stood knock-kneed, her hands trying to shield the large V of glistening pubic hair at her crotch, then ducked back into the bathroom and slammed the door.

I knocked on it hard and told her to come out.

The lock finally clicked, and the knob turned in my hand. I stepped back to let her pass. As she went by I breathed in her fragrant, wet smell. It saddened me. Her hair clung to her head, no longer a spiky crown. The robe had been thrown on hastily, drooping off one shoulder, the dark button of one nipple peeking out like the eye of a pet that had misbehaved. She plopped on the corner of the bed, sighing. The robe fell open further and she didn't bother to fix it.

Now I could see the catlike aspect of her face as a familial feature. Mexican royalty, or, at least, South Texas Mexican royalty. She rubbed her nose and let her hand fall in her lap, a balled-up fist, the red nails protruding like hard little daggers.

"I see you made it," she said. "Chicken dick."

There was a small rumble of clomping feet, and soon the room was crowded with uniforms. Lasko was trying to wedge his way through the throng, saying, "Hold on—hold on just a minute here."

An eager young officer stopped at the foot of the bed, gun drawn, handcuffs dangling. He looked down at the wet girl, then at the muddy, bloody bass player I saw in the mirror and said, "Which one of you is B. Q. Torres?"

"She is," said a voice. I turned around. It was Detective Watson, elbowing a couple of his men out of the way. He gave me an astringent smirk, whipped out his own handcuffs, and fastened them on her thin wrists. "You," he told her, "are under arrest for attempted murder."

She rolled her eyes, smirking. "Who says I did that?"

Watson grinned from ear to ear, looking back at me over his shoulder. "You'll find out later. Could be several people, though. Could be me, 'cause I think you did. Could be Roberto Villareal, for one. Or it could be Retha Thomas. She's starting to come around."

It turned out that parts of an Absolut bottle were embedded in my shoulder, a tooth was broken, and my leg needed stitches. Those things got me an escorted trip to Brackenridge Hospital, where I was sponged off, jabbed with needles, stitched, swabbed, probed, and bandaged. It took a few hours. Next to the Saturday night drug overdoses, car wreck and shooting victims, I was a low priority. A black officer kept an eye on me, even through the most embarrassing probes and sponges.

While they were putting on the finishing touches, Lasko came back and pulled up a chair, dismissing my sentinel. After they'd read Barbra Quiero Torres her rights and told her that her beloved daddy was dead, he said, she confessed.

"She was also pretty relieved that Retha is gonna be OK," said Lasko. "The two gals were pretty dang close, but this hot stud deejay by the name of Bone came between them. He was living with Retha, but he snuck over to Barbra's apartment one night for a quick one and Retha found out."

"Whoa," I interrupted. "Barbra told me *she* was going with a deejay, and *Retha* used to have a boyfriend named Bone."

Lasko shook his head. "There's only one deejay involved in

this case, and his name is Bone. He says he was living with Retha when he cheated on her with Barbra. The gals had a big falling out over it. Retha knew all about Barbra's daddy's troubles back here, and heard about the rumors going around about Vick, how it was that he 'helped out' guys when they needed it. After she got here, she got to the bottom of those rumors. Turns out that Vick has paid the emergency room bills for fourteen broken digits, six or seven broken arms, and five broken legs over the last ten years. And ten years is as far back as we've had time to check, so likely there's a lot more.''

I hung my head as a new wave of nausea swept over me. "Nice guy . . . end of an era . . ." I groaned, which caused the nurse to ask me if it was something she'd done. I shook my head and looked up at Lasko. "So Retha came out here to get even with Barbra for the boyfriend thing by blackmailing Bingo?"

He shrugged. "Partially, I guess. And she was trying to impress the IMF guy by volunteering to come out and check things out. When she got the goods on both Vick and Bingo, she thought she could parlay it into a job. She asked both Vick and Bingo for jobs, but they just tried to buy her off with a few hundred bucks. And you can guess that the IMF guy didn't have any further use for her, either.''

"And Barbra followed her out here once she got wind of things?" I said.

"Uh-huh. She claims she wasn't trying to kill her, she just got mad and flew into the proverbial rage. Said she was sick of people trying to put the bite on her dad, especially when it's her ex-best friend.''

"What does Retha say?"

"Nothing. She's opened her eyes and mumbled something. She recognizes her parents, and seems to understand that she's in a hospital. The doctors think she'll come out of it without too much damage, but it's real likely that she won't remember what happened. Retroactive amnesia, they call it.''

The nurse stepped back to admire her handiwork, handed

me some forms, and ducked out. Lasko gave me a grocery bag
with a pair of jeans and a T-shirt, both a few sizes too big. I
put them on and checked out at the ER desk, paying the bill
with the band's American Express card.

Retha was sleeping. The doctor said he thought she was going
to be all right, but it would take time. Her eyes were still rimmed
with black and yellow, her head sporting a turban of gauze.
But she was no longer in limbo. Soon she wouldn't need to be
hooked up to all the tubes and machines that were plugged into
her. Lasko and the doctor led me out to the hall once again.

"Her parents . . . ," I began.

The doctor shook his head. "Uh-uh," he said. "They're
asleep in a private room. First sleep they've had in a week, and
nobody, but nobody is going to disturb them."

An aide came padding up and said something about an emergency. The doctor shook my hand and trotted down the hall.
Lasko put an arm around me and told me that Monday morning
I'd have to have an interview with the DA, but not to worry
about it right now. First things first—Ladonna was in the waiting
room.

I went in there and we clung together like two sandburs. And
we stayed that way as Lasko drove us to her place. We stayed
that way for the better part of the day, and we stayed that way
all night too.

Monday morning the DA wanted me to look at two mug shots. At least one of the faces in the photos belonged to one of the two cowboys I'd given the $20,000 to in the parking lot of Rosie's Roadhouse, which is what I told the DA. Afterwards, he put the photos back in a folder, asked me to wait, and left the room. Fifteen minutes passed. A black female assistant came in looking like she'd been up all night with a sick child. She asked a lot of questions and took a lot of notes. Before she left, she made sure that she had a number where they could get in touch with me.

Lasko came in and plopped down in a chair, put his feet up, and got comfortable. "We got us a whole new case this morning," he said.

I was prepared for the worst. "Barbra's confession is inadmissible?"

"I don't think it's worth the paper it's written on," he said. "We don't have a shred of evidence to support it. Roberto, who I'll lay odds will never dance *conjunto* again, says it's bullshit. So does her mother, who flew in from LA with a hotshot lawyer last night. So does one blood-smudged partial print we got from the dresser and the blood that was under Retha's fingernails, neither of which match Barbra's."

"Whose do they match?"

"The man who did it, Bingo. Her dad."

"Are you sure?"

"Pretty dang sure. The first thing we showed ole Roberto after he come out of surgery yesterday was his spare blue lamé suit, all covered with Retha's blood. It was found stuffed in a minnow bucket down by the boat dock. Plus we got the cowboys that you just ID'd one of. They've worked for Bingo for almost ten years. Mostly down on his ranch near Beeville, but he used to fly them up here for special chores.

"Anyway, these folks are real talkative. Including the ex–Mrs. Torres, who is a damn good-looking six-foot blonde by the name of Cassandra Whitestone. What we know now is this: Bingo slipped out from surveillance Sunday night wearing Roberto's blue lamé suit, went to La Quinta, and waited for Retha."

"So he's the one who flew into the proverbial rage," I said.

He nodded grimly. "I doubt he knew exactly what he was gonna do when he went there. Probably figured to negotiate, because if he wanted to kill her, he'd have gotten someone else to do it."

"I just can't believe *anybody,* even Bingo, would stick around town as long as he did," I said, "waiting to see if Retha would either die or come to and say what happened. And then extort money from Vick. Twice."

"Aren't you the one heard him say he was entitled to the hundred grand since he paid for the records that earned Vick the money, only he couldn't step up and say so? That would've led the feds straight to the Danny Cortez alter ego. But that ain't the whole story. When we ran Danny Cortez through the FBI computer, we found a whole slew of things he was wanted for, and most of them wasn't nice."

"Would Vick know enough about those activities to testify about them?"

Lasko nodded. "You bet. And Bingo wouldn't like that, and not just because they used to be *business* partners."

"You mean Bingo and Vick . . ."

"They were pals, Martin. Why do you suppose Cassandra left Bingo back when the kid was just a tyke? She didn't like the class of people her husband was hanging around with. I'm not saying Bingo was a pervert, too, but he *knew*. And as the years went by and he flew in higher circles, he got used to the idea of looking down on it, pretending that he came from a different kind of stock. Maybe he even managed to forget the whole thing."

"But Retha reminded him," I said.

"Uh-huh. And Bingo flew into a rage when she threw that in his face on top of everything else."

"You think Barbra knows?"

"I don't think it would matter to her. She seems to think her dad hung the moon. I don't think she's too fond of her mom. She came out here to help Bingo. First Retha was in the way, then you."

"So what'll happen to her?"

"Who knows? We might have a case of obstructing justice and accessory to attempted murder if we can show she aided her dad in the attempted murder cover-up. We still have to sort out the extortion thing with Vick. Hell, we don't know for sure that she *didn't* meet up with Bingo to wait for Retha. I don't know. Roberto says that Bingo came back just before dawn. Alone."

"But you've got Barbra's confession."

"She denies it now. Her lawyer says it's no good. Hell, he's half right. Retha's gonna live, and all of our evidence points to Bingo, and none of it points to Barbra. The lawyer's getting her sprung right now."

Lasko swung his boots off the table and looked down at his hands in his lap. Slowly, like a cloud breaking up under a summer breeze, a smile broke out on his tired face. Not a broad smile, but one that showed more than a glint of mischief.

"You look like a guy who just remembered he got laid last night," I said.

202 · JESSE SUBLETT

"Well," he drawled as he toyed with his notepad, "it's that born-again hardass, Watson."

"Son of a Texas Ranger."

"He's whimpering like a whupped pup. He was so proud of getting that confession. He personally transcribed and photo-copied it, everything but tie it up with a little pink ribbon. Meanwhile I was on the horn to LA tracking down her mom and the dark past of Danny Cortez. And it was a couple of my boys that found that suit in that minnow bucket."

"Who's the Lieutenant's fair-haired boy now?"

He snorted. "I don't give a rat's ass about that. I'm not brown nosing for a desk job. I just wanna catch criminals and play a little bass guitar on the side." His grin widened as he tapped his notepad on the table. A wallet-sized photo fluttered out. He slipped it back inside without looking at it, but not before I saw whose gray-blue eyes, short black hair, and wide, rubbery mouth were on it.

"She loved the hell out of her dad," he said. "And when she gave her confession she was just as sweet as can be. But once we told her that her mother was flying in she cussed like oil field trash and turned cold as a witch. She's thrown a monkey wrench into this case from day one, and she's bound and de-termined to make it as hard on us as she can for as long as she can. Of that I'm certain. Man, she's one tough baby."

"Yeah. So is Retha."

He grinned and scratched his beard. "Oh, hell yes, that's a fact."

We stood up and shook hands. Lasko said that someone was there to give me a ride. It turned out to be Leo.

# 27

Leo got another Carta Blanca out of my refrigerator and opened it. He took a long pull from it and sat down, gathering courage. "It's a shame it wasn't the A & R guy," he said.

"Yeah," I said. "It would have made sense, wouldn't it?"

He almost smiled. "Damn right it'd make sense. Payola they probably figure they could fight, but if word got out they were making deals with perverts, hoo-boy, look out. Call the window-peeper brigade. But hell, record companies don't know shit about making sense, otherwise you and me woulda been made famous a long time ago."

He looked like he wanted to cry but had forgotten how.

"I appreciate your putting up with me," he said.

"You and Nadine working things out?"

"I don't know. She's still over at her mom's place. If we sort this thing out, she'll come back. If not, well, I gotta look for a place to flop. So, you still wanna play with me, or you fed up, or what?"

"Leo—"

"Nadine was seeing this guy while we were on the road," he abruptly blurted. "It didn't have to be a big deal, cause I haven't always been one hundred percent faithful to her. And to make matters worse, I never could seem to hide it from her. I don't know, she can read minds or something. Anyway, what she didn't know, the guy works with an old friend of mine, and every time they saw each other, I knew about it. I kept in touch with him on the road."

"And those were the times you blew up?"

He nodded. "More or less. I couldn't deal with it, Martin. Whenever I heard about it, all I could think was how much I hated her guts. But I couldn't stop thinking about it, about her legs wrapped around some guy, his cum going inside her, her liking it, kissing him, smoking a cigarette afterwards. I couldn't get it out of my head. I still can't. I think maybe I really do hate her."

"Maybe you really do feel something else, too."

He just shrugged.

"Who'd you call more often on the road, the guy's friend or her?"

"Aw, come on, man. You just don't understand."

"Maybe I don't," I said. "And maybe you don't, either. What about the thing with Vick? How did that come about?"

"Aw hell." His voice wavered, his knees jerked. "I owed Vick some money. A lot of money." He looked up at me with his glassy eyes.

"Go on," I said.

He looked down at a spot on the rug and spoke slowly but deliberately, as if he was anxious to get the words out and be done with them. I listened closely. His voice was quiet and thin.

"I was drunk out of my mind and he kept the Cuervo flowing. I was so eat up with hate for Nadine that I hated myself. I wanted to hurt her, I wanted to hurt myself. But I didn't have the kind of guts or whatever it takes to slash my wrists. I tried to run out in front of a car earlier that night, but my feet just stuck to the pavement. I went to that party, and it seemed like I was the only one there who wasn't having a good time. Ed gave me a ride that ended up over at the store. Vick kept the Cuervo flowing, kept talking with that singsong voice of his. It was like he wasn't really saying anything, not really, but it all made sense. In other words . . . it lulled me. That and the Cuervo, and I was tired. Crazy tired. Everything was a big blur, just one low moan. Like a machine, almost, just chugging away, and I was just pasted to the side of it. They beat me up. I swear, I don't think I felt a thing when he broke my hand. It was all in slow motion, like a dream. Afterwards, I guess Vick felt bad, and he gave me that guitar."

He swallowed hard and inhaled shakily, as if whatever he'd just swallowed had cut his insides. "God, I'm sorry. You won't tell anybody, will you?"

I put an arm around him and squeezed. No, I said, I wouldn't tell anybody. We finished our beers.

"Leo," I said finally, "I just wish you would have said something about this a long time ago. I feel like hell because you were going through hell while we were on the road and we didn't do anything about it."

"You did the best thing you could have done. You were there, and you didn't cut me loose. I just wanna play the blues, man. If I didn't get to play, I'd go all the way crazy. You're not gonna cut me loose now, are you?"

I shook my head. "I'd like to keep the band together. I don't want to look for another guitar player. I won't be responsible for you going all the way crazy, but I won't put up with any drugs, trashing motel rooms, or arson in the dressing room. Or anything else that's incredibly stupid."

The shadow of a grin played at the corners of his mouth like a threat. "Lay down the bottom line, bassman." We shook hands. "By the way, Ray told me to tell you he's available."

"I hoped he'd come around," I said. "When did you talk to him?"

"At the police station. He and Kate were on their way to Katz's for steak and eggs around seven o'clock yesterday morning after one of his after-hours gigs and they saw all the patrol cars in front of Vick's place. So he went down and told them a little story about him and Vick and apples."

"Apples?"

He nodded. "Way it goes, back when Ray first moved here from Lubbock and didn't have a gig and didn't know anybody, he ran into old Vick and Vick got him off to one side and offered him two hundred dollars to throw a bushel of apples at his butt."

"You're kidding."

"Nope."

"I wish I could've seen that," I said. "I'll bet he lost his cool for once."

"Well, that's just the thing. Like I said, Ray was new in town and he didn't know nobody and nobody knew him and he didn't have a gig. He needed the money."

I couldn't help laughing. Leo almost laughed too. "Oh, man," I said. "What a band."

Ladonna and I were stretched out on a blanket, watching Michael skip stones off the glassy surface of the creek. Not many people knew about my favorite secluded spot on Barton Creek, and we had it all to ourselves that afternoon. It was peaceful enough to get some thinking done, maybe even enough to stop thinking for a while.

I knew several clerks at the Hyatt who would either know or be able to find out if Barbra had been out of her room during the time of Retha's attack. But Lasko or Watson would get to them soon enough and put the matter to rest. It wasn't that I was harboring any illusions about Barbra. I was just sick of the whole deal.

I rested my head in Ladonna's lap and stared up at the big open sky, thinking about guilt and responsibility. It didn't take a genius to see that the private vexations of Vick and Leo and all the other Leos out there had branched out and hurt Retha Thomas. The quiet conspiracy that let Vick go for all those years had to share the guilt. They were as responsible for causing her pain as the crowd below a ledge hugger taunting him to jump, as guilty as the people who walk on by, too wrapped up in themselves to give a damn.

How guilty was I? As guilty as some, I supposed, but not as

guilty as others. I didn't feel like a hero, that's for sure. All I did was get in the way for a while, get used for a while, then fight back. I'd crippled one man for life, caused one to be shot to death, and chased another until he smashed up on a road-block and lost his head. I didn't feel too bad about it. Maybe I would someday, but right then I just felt lucky. Somebody loved me, I lived in Texas, and I had a working band that, although it wasn't the most stable one in the world, sure had some depth to it.

"Martin," said a low, smoky voice above me.

I opened my eyes. She was as beautiful as the sunny spring day.

"You've been talking to yourself," she said. "Shut up and kiss me and rub some lotion on my back."

Our lips met. We rolled off the blanket into the soft grass. Birds tweeted. Wind blew. When the sun went down, we went to her place.